Beach Blanket Barbie
By
Kathi Daley

This book is a work of fiction. Names, characters, places, and incidents either are products of the author's imagination or are used fictitiously. Any resemblance to actual events or locales or persons, living or dead, is entirely coincidental.

Copyright © 2014 by Katherine Daley

Version 1.0

All rights reserved, including the right of reproduction in whole or in part in any form.

This book is dedicated to my beach-loving boys, Isaiah, Eisley, and Greyson.

Special thanks to all my Facebook friends who show their support by sharing their opinions and encouragement. I also want to thank my team of advance readers for taking time out of their busy lives to help me launch each new book. I'd like to offer special thanks to Amy Brantley for her help with EVERYTHING up to and including the recipes for this episode of the Zoe Donovan story.

And, as always, love and thanks to my sister Christy for her time, encouragement, unwavering support, and valuable feedback. I also want to thank Carrie, Cristin, and Danny for the Facebook shares, Ricky for the webpage, Randy Ladenheim-Gil for the editing, and, last but not least, my super-husband Ken for allowing me time to write by taking care of everything else.

Books by Kathi Daley

Buy them on Amazon today.

Paradise Lake Series:
Pumpkins in Paradise
Snowmen in Paradise
Bikinis in Paradise
Christmas in Paradise
Puppies in Paradise – *February 2015*

Zoe Donovan Mysteries:
Halloween Hijinks
The Trouble With Turkeys
Christmas Crazy
Cupid's Curse
Big Bunny Bump-off
Beach Blanket Barbie
Maui Madness
Derby Divas
Haunted Hamlet
Turkeys, Tuxes, and Tabbies
Christmas Cozy – *November 2014*
Alaskan Alliance – *December 2014*

Road to Christmas Romance:
Road to Christmas Past

Chapter 1

Friday, May 16

"Zoe, you have to do something," Bitzy Bellingham said, just a tad too loudly to be considered prim and proper.

"I really think it's best to let them finish," I suggested to the polished woman with professionally styled hair, designer clothes, and impeccable makeup.

"But poor Muffet must be traumatized," Bitzy insisted as she paced back and forth in three-inch heels that were definitely not meant for everyday wear.

I looked across the yard, where Bitzy's prizewinning bichon frise was having *relations* with a stray dog who had dug his way in under the fence. I seriously doubted Muffet was traumatized, given the fact that she had climbed up onto one of the steps leading to the heated pool to provide enough height for her much taller suitor to perform his manly deed. Still, I was in charge of animal control and rehabilitation for my hometown of Ashton Falls. I suppose it was reasonable that Bitzy called me with the expectation that I could somehow fix the rather awkward situation.

"Muffet will be fine," I assured Bitzy. "I realize you're concerned for her, but I assure you that things aren't as bad as they seem. As soon as they're finished, I'll catch Casanova and take him to the Zoo."

"'Aren't as bad as they seem'? Are you kidding me? This is the most horrible thing that could have happened."

"I don't know that it's the *most* horrible thing. Muffet doesn't seem to have been harmed in any way, and if you ask me, she seems to have a thing for her suitor. Look, she's smiling."

"She's not smiling," Bitzy disagreed. "Muffet was supposed to be mated to a champion stud and this mongrel ruined everything."

"The heart wants what the heart wants," I reminded Bitzy.

"Oh dear lord. I can assure you that Muffet does *not* have feelings for that filthy, mangy mutt with half an ear. This is simply a disaster, and it's your job, Zoe Donovan, to do something to fix it."

"You know," I tried to sound encouraging, "our Casanova sort of looks like Tramp from *Lady and the Tramp.* I've seen the movie, and everything turns out okay."

"This is not a movie," Bitzy insisted. "Now, I insist you do your job and break this up. Immediately!"

"Looks like they're done anyway." I unwound the leash I was carrying and approached the trespassing dog, who seemed mellow and cooperative by this point. He really was a sweet thing, with a look of mischief in his intelligent eyes. He was covered in long, matted fur that was so dirty it was hard to tell its true color, but I suspected his coat was a lighter shade of the curly brown fur that covered his ears. I was reaching down to snap on the lead when he darted to his left, then took off back toward the fence he'd crawled under in the first place.

"You let him go," Bitzy exclaimed.

"I didn't let him go," I said. I knelt down to see if the little scamp was still on the other side of the fence, but it appeared he was long gone.

"You should have grabbed him right off," Bitzy informed me. "Now we'll never get him."

"Don't worry, I'll track him down." I turned back toward Bitzy and cringed. It appeared that in his eagerness to make his way into the yard, our Casanova had dug up one of Bitzy's prized roses. I knew the only things Bitzy cared more about than her pampered little dog were her pampered long-stemmed roses. At least it was too early for them to have bloomed. Maybe she wouldn't notice them until after I left.

"Well, that was a total waste of a stud fee," Bitzy complained. "I spent months researching the perfect pairing for my Muffet and it's all for naught. I suppose I'll need to terminate the pregnancy and start again in six months. Maybe the owner of the stud I selected will transfer the deposit, since services were never rendered."

"No!" I shouted, louder than I should have.

"No what?" Bitzy looked confused by my outburst.

"Don't end the pregnancy, if there even *is* a pregnancy. These things don't always take, you know."

"Yes, I know that, but a mixed-breed litter is totally worthless to me, so why bother with the hassle and expense of letting the pregnancy run its course?"

"Because," I argued, "you might end up with a really exceptional puppy. You know Charlie?"

Charlie, my mixed-breed dog, was waiting for me in the truck.

"Of course. Everyone in town knows Charlie."

"And you like him?"

"Of course I like him. Sweet little thing sat with me for hours when I was in the hospital last year with my broken leg."

For those of you who don't know, Charlie is a therapy dog.

"Charlie is the product of a pairing much like this. My mom's friend had a prizewinning Tibetan terrier who had an unfortunate encounter with a mystery dog, resulting in Charlie. If Muffet *is* pregnant, and she may not be," I assured Bitzy, "please let her deliver the pups. I'll reimburse you for all your expenses and take the puppies off your hands the minute they're weaned."

Bitzy frowned but appeared to be considering my proposal. "You'll pay for all the expenses?"

"I will."

"Even if Muffet needs a C-section, which is likely, given the size of the mongrel who covered her?"

"Yes, even then."

"I'll need to consult with my vet."

"Certainly. I encourage you to do so."

Bitzy picked up Muffet, who immediately began to struggle to get down. I smiled at the hyper little dog, who looked at me with soulful eyes, as if begging me to rescue her from a life of structure and propriety. I suspected the pampered pooch had few opportunities to let loose and really be a dog. By the look of her manicure—pink polish with sparkles, I'm not kidding—and perfectly groomed coat, I suspected she spent more time at the beauty parlor than playing in the yard. Bitzy took a few steps toward the mansion she lived in before turning back and speaking to me. "I'm not sure that carrying a litter of half-breeds will be the best thing for poor Muffet, but I promise I'll think about it."

"That's all I can ask. For now, I suggest you isolate Muffet until she is out of estrus."

"Yes, I guess that might be a good idea."

After looking around the area for some sign of Scamp, which was the name I'd given the dog, I headed back toward town. Charlie stuck his head out of the window as we merged onto the highway that ran along the lake. It was a perfect summer day. The midday sun shimmered on the surface of the glassy water, which was so perfectly calm you could see the mountains reflecting on its surface. The weatherman was calling for temperatures in the midseventies, and I couldn't help but feel a song in my heart. Charlie and I headed to Ellie's Beach Hut for lunch on the pier, as planned. As I pulled onto Main Street, I rolled down my window and let the warm afternoon breeze blow thorough my long brown curls. I was beginning to regret my choice of heavy denim jeans rather than the knee-length khaki shorts I normally wore to work during the warm summer months. At least I'd pulled on a tank top under my Zoe's Zoo sweatshirt, which I'd discarded shortly after leaving Bitzy's hillside home.

I slowed down in deference to the hundreds of tourists wandering aimlessly along the sidewalk of the small downtown section of Ashton Falls. Men, women, and children dressed in shorts and tank tops combed the cute mom-and-pop shops looking for that special trinket to take home from their trip to the mountain resort. I slowed my truck to a good ten miles an hour below the posted speed limit of twenty-five and relaxed as the sun hit my left arm, which was propped on the open window of the driver's side door. Bon Jovi blared from the radio as I took in the warm-weather frenzy of our little town.

Charlie barked in greeting as Hazel Hampton, the town librarian, waved at us from the sidewalk in front of Rosie's Café, where she was talking to Willa Walton, a member of the Events Committee to which we both belonged. Each month the committee organized and planned an event we hoped would bring tourists from the valley to our little hamlet to spend their hard-earned money in our local shops. As the snow from the long winter melted and the focus on skiing gave way to the outdoor sports that can be found on our white-sand beaches and large alpine lake, the events we orchestrated moved outdoors as well. Next on the agenda was the four-day Memorial Day event, which featured sailboat races and water-ski demonstrations for the outdoor enthusiasts, a kiddie carnival and sand castle–building competition for the younger crowd, and a beer crawl and outdoor music and arts festival for those over twenty-one. I was in charge of the kiddie carnival, which would be set up in the park on the east end of town, as well as the pet adoption clinic my assistant Jeremy and I had decided to sponsor in the hopes of placing the plethora of puppies and kittens we seemed to acquire every spring.

Although Memorial Day was still a week away, the town was filled to the brim with visitors from the valley who couldn't wait to spend time on the water. I groaned as I pulled into the parking area that served the businesses on the pier as well as the most popular beach in the area. You see, I drive a truck—a big one—and parking is a problem more often than not. There was no way I could squeeze into one of the few spots left, so I executed a twenty-point turn and returned to the highway, after which I made a quick left, which took me to the alleyway behind the downtown shops. I found an empty space behind Bears and Beavers and parked. I decided that I really should let Gilda Reynolds, the owner of the eclectic little shop, know that I'd parked in one of the four spots designated for her business, so I clipped a leash on Charlie and headed inside via the delivery door at the back of the building.

"Zoe, what brings you and Charlie in on this beautiful day?" Gilda greeted us.

I explained about the truck, and she assured me that she was working alone that afternoon, so I could leave my monster of a vehicle there as long as I liked.

"Has business been good?" I asked politely as Gilda unpacked beaver cookie jars.

"Business has been outstanding. The beautiful weather has brought beachcombers from miles around. I completely sold out of those coffee mugs I bought a few months ago."

"It really has been perfect weather ever since that freak snow we had last month," I agreed.

"Can Charlie have a biscuit?" Gilda asked.

"Certainly," I answered as Gilda made her way to a cabinet behind the cash register. Gilda is a short woman with a stocky frame, green eyes, and a bright red afro. I suspect that the color of her hair comes from a box rather than her genetics, although in all the years I've known her, she's never altered the shade or made any attempt to tame her curls.

"How is Hershey doing?" I asked. Hershey is a chocolate lab Gilda adopted a while back. The dog is a sweet thing with a laundry list of emotional problems that Gilda and I have been working to remedy. Initially, he suffered severe separation anxiety whenever Gilda left her alone, but after we introduced a second lab—a yellow female named Honey—to the family, Hershey seemed to calm down.

"She's doing wonderfully. All of her behavior issues have disappeared since Honey joined the family."

"I'm glad it worked out. Honey seemed like she'd be just the type of companion Hershey would relate to."

"By the way, I meant to tell you that your mom stopped in with Harper the other day. She's such a cute little thing, and you know, I think she's going to look at lot like her big sister. She definitely has your beautiful blue eyes, although she seems to have your mom's hair."

"Thankfully," I replied. While my hair is thick, curly, brown, and unmanageable, my mom has long blond hair that hangs perfectly straight, with little to no effort on her part. "And maybe she'll have my dad's height as well. Topping the height chart at five feet isn't always the thrill that some would assume."

"Preaching to the choir." Gilda laughed. Poor Gilda is a good two inches shorter than me. "When I first heard that your mom was back in town after all these years, I was afraid she might not stay, but she seemed wonderfully content in her role as mother."

"Yeah, I guess she's matured."

My mom is forty-two. While she may be a tad on the old side to be a new mother, she's settled right into her role during the month since Harper was born. I know there are those in town who remember my mother deserting me, leaving me in the custody of my father when I was just a few days old, but that was twenty-five years ago, and it seems things will be different this time around.

"Mom mentioned that you were asking about Sophie's puppies," I said, changing the subject.

Sophie was a short-timer from the Bryton Lake Shelter who'd been delivered to the Zoo in April. She was very pregnant at the time, so I'd taken her home, although my mom ended up adopting her and delivering her four pups. Since my dad already had two dogs and a cat, my parents had agreed that Mom would have to find homes for all four pups.

"Yeah. My sister's dog passed recently, and I thought of Sophie's pups. Your mom sure is being particular about who adopts the little guys."

I laughed. "She's taken the adoption process to a whole new level." I can be pretty picky when it comes to matching prospective animal parents with their new pets, but Mom has been almost manic about finding just the right placement for each of Sophie's pups. "How'd your sister do?" I wondered.

"I think she's in the running. Your mom wanted to visit her home, which I believe she plans to do next week."

"If your sister attends the Memorial Day event, come find me. I'll introduce her to Mom. I'm sure that will go a long way toward moving her to the top of the list."

"Speaking of Memorial Day," Gilda responded, "did you ever hear back from the vendor with the snow-cone machine for next weekend?"

"Yeah, but he was already booked," I answered. "I guess I should have anticipated there might be a conflict on a holiday weekend and made the call earlier. He recommended a man who does cotton candy and lemonade. I thought about contacting him, but I'm pretty sure the hot dog vendor does lemonade, and I didn't want to create any controversy by introducing two vendors with the same product."

"What about smoothies?" Gilda asked.

"Smoothies would be good. Do you have a contact?"

"Actually, I do." Gilda made her way to the office in the back of the store. She pulled up a file on her computer and then jotted down a phone number on a piece of scratch paper. "You should call right away," Gilda said. "He may already be booked, but it wouldn't hurt to try."

"Thanks, I'll do that," I promised as I slipped the paper into my pocket . . . where it remained until my pants went through the washer, but don't tell Gilda. "I'm heading over to the Beach Hut for lunch. If you need me to move the truck for some reason, just call my cell."

"Will do. It's a beautiful day to eat outdoors. Hopefully you'll be able to get a table."

"I'm sure I'll find something."

"I wasn't sure that little space on the pier would make a good place for an eatery when Ellie first announced her plans," Gilda commented, "but it seems like the place has been packed since the weather got nice. The only downside, I suppose, is that a lot of the parallel parking along Main Street is being taken up by folks going to the beach, now that the parking lot is full with diners for the restaurant."

"Yeah, I can see how that would be a problem," I sympathized.

"A few of the business owners are talking about initiating a petition to install parking meters along the main drag to discourage long-term parking."

I frowned. "I suppose I understand the intention, but parking meters don't really meld with the small-town charm we work hard to sell to the tourists who visit each year. Maybe we should look at a shuttle to take people from a lot that could be set up outside of town to the beach," I suggested.

"Most folks don't like the inconvenience of a shuttle," Gilda warned.

"Maybe we could offer an incentive to take the shuttle."

"Like what?"

"I don't know offhand, but it might be a good topic of discussion for the next events' meeting. I should get going. Can I bring you something from Ellie's?"

"A cold drink would be nice, if it isn't too much trouble."

"No trouble at all. I should be back this way in an hour or so."

Chapter 2

I stopped to say hi to several locals as I made my way across the street. When I saw the crowd on the pier, I began to wonder if I'd have to wait for a table, but just as I arrived, a couple I didn't know got up, and I slid into their place. The sun on my shoulders felt better than I can describe. I looked toward the beach, where a flock of kids chased each other, dodging to avoid a group of teens playing volleyball. There's something about those first days of summer, when the sun is warm and the lake is blue, that brings out the happy in people.

I knew that in another month the beach would be filled with brightly colored towels and umbrellas placed so close together you'd barely be able to find the smooth white sand. The beach situated across from the downtown section of Main Street, next to the pier, is the busiest on the lake. During the warmest summer months, the town sponsors a band on the pier that can be enjoyed from both the pier and the beach. The bands played during the late afternoon and early evening, providing a wonderful and festive setting from which to watch the always spectacular sunsets.

"Oh, good, you found a table," Ellie said, sitting down across from me.

"What's with the binoculars?" I asked the pretty brunette. Ellie had a pair hanging around her neck.

She smiled at me with her big brown eyes as she lifted them over her head and handed them to me. "Check out the woman lying just to the left of that red and white umbrella," she instructed.

I did as directed. There was a very tan woman wearing a red bikini lying on her stomach. "Yeah, so?"

"Guess who it is," Ellie encouraged.

"I have no idea; I can't see her face."

"Check out the tattoo on her right shoulder."

I focused the lenses so I could make out a small yet brightly colored butterfly. "Barbie," I gasped.

Barbie is our other best friend, Levi Denton's ex. After he broke up with her just before Valentine's Day, she turned into a bit of a psycho, damaging hundreds of dollars' worth of Levi's possessions, including his television and most of his clothing. She left shortly after that, and we figured we'd seen the last of her. Apparently, we were wrong.

"What is she doing back?" I wondered.

"I have no idea," Ellie answered. "I noticed her walking by a couple of hours ago and have been spying on her ever since."

"Aren't you supposed to be working?" I reminded her.

"I have extra staff today," Ellie explained. "I've been pitching in but still had time to spy. Levi is going to flip out when he hears she's back."

Ellie was right. Levi *was* going to flip out.

"Let me grab you a sandwich and then I'll fill you in. Can Charlie have some scraps from the kitchen?"

"Yeah, as long as it's unseasoned meat and veggies."

"I knew you were coming, so I've been keeping the best leftovers on the side. I'll be right back."

Ellie left the binoculars with me while she went back inside the tiny restaurant. Ellie's Beach Hut only recently opened, featuring a small but cozy interior with a soup-and-sandwich counter, a small wood-burning stove, and limited tables, as well as a large outdoor deck with an industrial-size BBQ and plenty of lakefront seating. From my table next to the railing that lined the pier, I had a bird's-eye view of Barbie as she soaked up some afternoon rays.

Barbie isn't just a beautiful woman, she's a *stunningly* beautiful woman. A small and extremely fit body, perfect skin, long blond hair, and huge blue eyes combine to create a vision that men everywhere—and some women, as well—can't help but stare at. Barbie knows her effect on men and uses it to her advantage by flirting with anyone and everyone she wants or needs something from. It wasn't just Levi who was going to flip out when the news of Barbie's return hit the Ashton Falls gossip network; most of the women in town were going to be less than happy as well.

"Ham and cheese sub okay?" Ellie asked as she placed a plate with the sandwich accompanied by her famous potato salad and a diet soda on the table in front of me, along with a plate with leftovers, which she put on the ground for Charlie.

"Ham is fine," I answered as Charlie licked Ellie's hand in gratitude for the treat. "So fill me in on your morning entertainment."

"Barbie showed up at around ten-thirty with lifeguard guy."

"Lifeguard guy?"

"That's what I've been calling the guy in the red board shorts sitting under the umbrella Barbie is lying next to."

I used the binoculars to check out the guy Ellie was referring to. He did sort of look like a lifeguard with his dark tan and shaggy hair. "So they're together?" I confirmed.

"They arrived together and are sitting together, but they don't seem to be a couple," Ellie clarified.

"How can you tell?"

"Because when Conan came over and kissed Barbie full on the lips, lifeguard guy didn't seem to care."

"Conan?"

"Look to Barbie's left and up a few rows. You'll see a huge man with dark hair and dark swim trunks who looks like Conan the Barbarian."

I did as instructed. "You mean the guy sitting next to the blonde in the yellow bikini?"

"Yeah, that's him."

"And yellow bikini didn't care that her caveman kissed another woman?"

"She hadn't arrived yet, although once she did, she made Conan move his towel away from his original position, just behind Barbie."

I laughed. "It looks like nothing has changed. Men are still falling all over our former yoga instructor and women are still busily running interference."

"That's not the half of it." Ellie giggled. "Lisa and Jason Grover came by shortly after Conan and his girlfriend moved. Jason just glanced at Barbie and Lisa slapped him, turned around, and headed back toward the parking lot."

The rumor mill had reported a short-lived affair between Barbie and Jason last summer, although I'm not sure anyone had proof of such a deed. "What did Jason do?" I asked.

"He took off after his wife."

"Sounds like you've had quite a show."

"I saved the best for last." Ellie was grinning.

"Do tell."

"Another man stopped by to speak to the fabulous B. At first I thought maybe Barbie was in trouble, until I noticed her run one of her perfectly manicured fingernails across his chest before she stood on tiptoe to rub seductively against his body while whispering in his ear."

"Whose ear did she whisper into?" I had to admit I was getting hooked on Ellie's story.

"Sheriff Salinger."

"No!" I gasped. "Salinger is a married man *and* a good twenty years older than Barbie."

"They seemed pretty familiar with each other from where I was sitting."

"Was Salinger here in his uniform?"

When Ellie first mentioned that Barbie had run her finger across someone's chest, I'd been picturing a naked chest, which is what most men sport at the beach, but once she revealed the identity of the individual on the receiving end of the gesture, I really hoped I'd misunderstood. The thought of Salinger in nothing but swim trunks left a sour taste in my mouth, and I hated to waste the lunch Ellie had prepared.

"Yeah, he was in uniform. I think he was doing parking-lot patrol and noticed Barbie on the beach."

"Wow. Salinger and Barbie. She must have done something pretty serious to be willing to shack up with Salinger."

"What do you mean?" Ellie asked.

"I mean, the only reason I can comprehend why Barbie would give Salinger the time of day would be if she'd gotten herself into big-time trouble and was using her wiles to convince him to give her a pass."

"Yeah, I guess I see your point."

"Uh-oh," I gasped. "It looks like Barbie is headed our way."

"Hide the binoculars," Ellie said, panicked.

I looked around, but there was nowhere to hide them, so I tossed them into the garbage can near the table and hoped no one would toss anything really messy inside before we could retrieve them.

"Well, if it isn't the annoying duo," Barbie greeted us. The woman hadn't even bothered to slip on shorts or a wrap, and her bikini was about as small as a bikini could be.

"What brings you to town?" I asked.

"Business."

"Will you be staying long?" Ellie inquired.

"Long enough." Barbie looked bored by the conversation. "I heard you have frozen drinks at your bar."

"We do," Ellie confirmed. "What can I get you?"

"Something with rum. Make it two."

Ellie walked over to the outdoor bar and gave Barbie's order to the bartender.

"So I heard your mom got knocked up," Barbie said as she waited for her drink.

"I have a new baby sister," I answered as politely as I could.

"A couple of people told me that your mom moved back to town to raise the kid."

"Yes," I replied. "She did."

"Doesn't that bug you?"

Bug me? "Why would it bug me?" I asked.

"Your old lady dumps you on your dad's doorstep like an unwanted kitten when you were a baby, but from what I've heard, she's gone all maternal over little sis. Seems like it would sting a bit."

Actually, it did at times, but I'd never admit that to Barbie or anyone else. "No," I responded. "It doesn't bother me at all. I love Harper and am glad that my mom has decided to stay around to raise her."

"Your drinks should be right up," Ellie interrupted, thank God.

"Nice rock," Barbie commented on Ellie's engagement ring.

"Thank you," Ellie responded politely.

"So when's the big day?" Barbie asked.

"We haven't set a date yet, but Rob and I are thinking that maybe sometime over the summer would be nice."

"You know what's funny?" Barbie got a distant look on her face. "A guy breaks up with a girl because he's in love with someone else, but when the girl comes back to town, she finds out the someone else who broke the couple up is engaged to some totally random guy."

I nodded at Ellie not to say anything. I knew Barbie was right about the reason Levi broke up with her, and I also knew Ellie would deny it. Barbie and Ellie never had gotten along, and the last thing I nccdcd was to have to break up a chick fight.

"Your drinks are ready," Ellie announced without responding to Barbie's statement. "And they're on the house."

"Thanks, that's very nice."

Barbie took the drinks and returned to the beach. "What a witch," Ellie commented as she walked away. "Do you think she was talking about me?"

"You know she was."

"And do you think she's right? Do you think Levi broke up with Barbie because of me?"

I hesitated. Opening up that can of worms would be awkward, but I couldn't very well lie to my best friend. "What do you think?" I asked instead of answering.

Ellie got a distant look on her face, as if she was considering the idea. "I guess I thought Levi just got tired of Barbie, like he does every girl he goes out with. He mentioned she wanted a commitment, and he wasn't ready for that sort of thing. I never considered the situation beyond that."

"Look, I don't think the reason Levi broke up with Barbie is all that important. He did break up with her, and from what we've seen, it was a good thing he did. The girl is a psycho. I say we forget about Barbie, who will more than likely be gone in a few days, and get back to enjoying this fantastic weather."

"Yeah," Ellie agreed. "You're right. Are we still on for tonight?"

My boyfriend Zak and I were having a party at his lakefront estate.

"We are," I confirmed.

"Can I bring anything?"

"Just a swimsuit if you want to swim."

"Sounds like fun. I bought Hannah a life vest," Ellie informed me. "Rob thought it would be a good idea if she wanted to swim, and she loves the water. I think she's going to be a real fish when she grows up."

"Have you thought about swim lessons?" I asked.

"She's only two."

"It's never too early to get kids started," I reminded Ellie. "Kids seem to have a natural comfort in the water that tends to turn to fear if you don't introduce them early enough. I learned to swim almost before I could walk. You should talk to Rob about it."

"Yeah, I will."

"I guess Charlie and I should get back to the Zoo." Charlie looked up at me and tilted his head when he heard his name. He'd finished off Ellie's snack and had settled in the shade to take a nap while Ellie and I visited. "I need to check on the bobcat kitten that's due to arrive today."

"Seems like you're getting a full house. Is room going to be an issue?"

"Eventually. We have four bear cubs now, as well as four coyote pups and now the bobcat. Thanks to the remodel, we still have a few empty wild animal pens. The domestic animal pens are only about half full, so we could put some of our wildlife in the larger pens temporarily if we have to."

"I heard you got in a bunch of puppies and kittens."

"A bunch," I confirmed.

"I've been thinking about getting Hannah a kitten after Rob and I are married. She really wants one, but Rob doesn't want to have to take care of it."

"Just let me know when you want it and I'll find the perfect one for Hannah. Are you still considering July?"

I knew Ellie wanted to get married on the beach in front of Zak's estate at some point during the summer, but here it was the middle of May and she'd yet to set a date.

"Yeah, July or August. I guess we really should decide."

"Yeah, you should. It'll take time to line up food and music. Besides, you'll want to go off the mountain and shop for a dress. We can make a girls' weekend out of it."

"Sounds fun. I'll talk to Rob over the weekend. I know I really wanted a summer wedding, but fall is nice too."

I looked at Ellie. "Are you having second thoughts?"

"Second thoughts? Why would I have second thoughts?"

"Because you were only sort of sure this was the right thing for you in the first place, and now you seem to be avoiding the issue of setting a date."

"I'm not having second thoughts; it's just that when I think about setting a date, my chest starts to hurt and I feel like I can't breathe."

"Sounds like second thoughts to me."

"I just need a chance to get used to the idea. Getting married is a huge deal, and everything happened so fast. I'm sure once we set a date, I'll feel less stressed about the whole thing."

"Yeah." I hugged Ellie in a show of support. "I'm sure you will."

Charlie sat up and barked at the sound of someone yelling in the distance. I released Ellie and stood back to see if I could locate the source of the voice. A woman with yellow bikini bottoms—only bottoms—was standing next to the towel she'd been lying on with one arm across her chest and the other pointing down the beach. I looked that way and noticed a dog that looked an awful lot like Scamp heading from the beach into the forest behind the beach with a yellow bikini top trailing from his mouth.

"I gotta go," I said to Ellie, before calling Charlie to my side and heading at a steady jog in the direction in which I'd seen Scamp disappear.

Chapter 3

Saturday, May 17

Despite the fact that it had been a late night, Charlie and I woke up early and decided to go for a run. Zak was still asleep, and Lambda, loyal dog that he is, refused to leave his side. It seemed that things had been so hectic of late, Charlie and I hadn't enjoyed our runs on the beach as often as we once had. It was a beautiful morning, with the blue sky and bright sunshine that promised another warm day. Although the temperatures were supposed to climb into the midseventies once again, the overnight temps had dipped into the thirties, so the beach was empty in the early morning. As I jogged along the sand that stretched from the cove where Zak's home and my boathouse both resided to the main part of the lake and the larger public beaches, I thought about the day ahead.

I'd left Zak a note telling him that I planned to go home to my boathouse to shower after my run. Most times Zak stayed over with me because I had my cats, Marlow and Spade, to consider, but with the party at Zak's lasting until the wee hours of the morning, it seemed easier to stay at his place. During the weeks my mom had lived with Zak, I'd pretty much moved in with the two of them, so we'd brought Marlow and Spade to Zak's, but last night most of the ten exterior doors to Zak's mansion had been open, creating a dangerous situation for felines living in an environment filled with coyotes and other large carnivores.

I planned to head back into town to meet up with Levi after I cleaned up. Levi and I had both been asked to participate in the ski and wakeboard demonstrations that were being held the following weekend, and the whole water-sports team planned to meet to go over the choreography for the event. Two of Zak's business buddies who lived in Hawaii were in Ashton Falls on vacation, so Zak had invited them to go sailing while I was tied up. Later that evening, Zak and I planned to have dinner at my parents' so we could visit my brand-new baby sister. I supposed Ellie would have to work today. It was hard opening a new business. Luckily, I had my assistant manager, Jeremy Fisher, as well as new hires Tiffany Middleton, Bobby Evans, and Tank and Gunner Rivers to help out. With my new staff, I rarely worked weekends unless there was a pet adoption clinic or some other special event.

As I left the beach that bordered the lake in my little cove for the wide-open sand of the larger body of water encompassing the main part of the lake, I focused on the memory of the night before. After our guests left, I'd been heading up the stairs toward Zak's big bed when he suggested a moonlight swim in his heated pool as a way of winding down before we turned in. He'd built a fire in the stone fireplace that was located next to the indoor/outdoor pool. The flicker from the fire as it reflected on the water created a feeling of luxury and romance that had to be experienced to be truly appreciated.

We'd drifted on our backs and looked at the stars as Zak shared plans for the future and dreams as yet unrealized. I knew Zak hoped we could make our relationship more permanent in the upcoming months, but for reasons I don't understand myself, every time Zak mentions a more permanent living arrangement, I find myself changing the subject to avoid the discussion.

With the romantic atmosphere Zak had created, it wasn't too hard to divert his attention away from cohabitation and toward more immediate needs and desires. Zak wrapped me in one of his huge towels and carried me up to his bed, where we enjoyed our love for each other well into the night. The memory of our night together made me consider discontinuing my run in favor of turning around and heading back for another round, but then I saw the pier in the distance. Somehow the arrival of a destination gave me the incentive I needed to keep going. The pier was actually another two miles away, but the day was bright and the visibility perfect, making the wooden structure appear much closer. As I neared the pier, I noticed something floating in the water. I slowed to a walk and took a closer look. It was something red. It looked like . . . *oh, crap; not again.*

The first thing I noticed when I entered Sheriff Salinger's office and sat down across the desk from him was that he appeared to be detached, unaffected by the news that Barbie Bennington had drowned. Based on the display Ellie had witnessed the previous day, I expected the man to be a little more upset. If I didn't know better, I'd assume Salinger and the dead yoga instructor had never even met, yet the display Ellie had told me about suggested a relationship with a certain level of intimacy.

"I need you to tell me everything you observed this morning," Salinger said, beginning the familiar song and dance. It really is mind-blowing how often I've been in this office having the exact same discussion with the man across the desk from me in the past few months. Luckily, Salinger had requested that one of his men drive me home to change into dry clothes before bringing me down to the station.

"Charlie and I were jogging and saw something in the water, under the pier. We stopped to take a look and recognized the floating object to be a body. I called you, kicked off my shoes, dove in, and pulled the body to the beach. I considered mouth-to-mouth, but it was evident it was way too late for that."

"Yes, I'm afraid it was. Initial reports put the time of death at between eleven p.m. last night and one a.m. this morning."

"Have you confirmed that the cause of death was drowning?"

"It looks like that was the case. We believe she may have been drunk and simply fallen off the pier into the water."

I frowned. "There's a railing around the pier," I pointed out.

"True, but it's easily scaled."

"Suggesting that she climbed over the railing and jumped in . . . Barbie doesn't seem the type to drink in excess or to engage in late-night swimming either."

"Why do you say that?" Salinger asked.

"For one thing, she was very weight-conscious. In all the time I've known her, I've never seen her have more than a single cocktail."

"Maybe last night was a special event," Salinger suggested.

"Perhaps. But Barbie was wearing a very expensive dress that is in no way washable. I don't see her voluntarily jumping into the lake, and with the railing, she couldn't have simply stumbled, which leaves . . ."

"You think someone pushed her," Salinger concluded.

"It makes the most sense."

"If she fell against the railing, she could have had enough momentum to tumble over," Salinger pointed out.

"I suppose. It seems unlikely, though."

"Prior to finding her body, were you aware that Ms. Bennington was back in town?" Salinger asked.

"Yes. I saw her yesterday while I was having lunch at the Beach Hut."

"Did you speak to her?"

"Briefly. She came up from the beach to get a cold drink."

"Did she mention why she was here?"

It might be my imagination, but Salinger seemed tense when he asked that particular question.

"No. She didn't say much at all, actually."

"Was she with anyone?"

I thought about it. I didn't actually see Barbie with anyone other than lifeguard guy, so I decided to keep Ellie's confidence and not mention the others. "When she came up to the pier she was alone," I answered, "but there was a man sitting in the chair under the umbrella she appeared to be using. I assume they were together."

"And did you recognize this man?"

"No. I suppose he could be a visitor to the area."

Salinger jotted down some notes. "Can you describe the man?"

"Dark hair, tan, seemed fit. He was wearing red board shorts. I really wasn't close enough to pick out details such as eye color, and he never stood up while I was there, so I couldn't guess at height."

"And what time would you say it was when you saw Ms. Bennington?"

I shrugged. "I guess around twelve-thirty."

"Okay, that should do it." Salinger closed his notebook.

"Really? 'Cause I can think of additional questions you might want to ask me."

"I think we're done for now."

Weird.

"Okay," I said. "I guess you know where to find me."

After assuring Zak that I was totally fine and planned to get together with Levi and the others as planned, he decided to go ahead and go sailing with his friends. I know that may sound cold on my part, but there wasn't much I could do, and I had a feeling Levi might need a friend. I'd called and told him what happened, and while he'd tried to sound unaffected, I could tell the whole thing had derailed him more than he was letting on. Levi is a sensitive man with a big heart, and he'd once had some pretty strong feelings for Barbie. While he had broken things off with her and hadn't appeared to have missed her all that much in the interim, I knew Levi's feelings ran deep.

"You know, Barbie called me," Levi informed me as we sat on the beach, waiting for a few stragglers to show up. Somehow the beauty of the afternoon didn't match the melancholy mood that had descended upon us.

"She did?" I waited as my best friend looked out toward the sand, his long brown hair hanging in his eyes.

"Thursday morning." Levi looked up at me with eyes as blue as my own. "She said she was in town and really needed to see me. I was being a jerk and totally blew her off, even when she said it was important. Now I have to wonder if her death is in some way my fault."

"What do you mean, your fault?"

"What if she was in trouble? What if I could have helped her if I'd let go of my pride and agreed to meet with her? She said she needed help. I shouldn't have told her to get lost. I should have helped."

Poor Levi. He did have a point.

"You had a reason not to want to see her," I reminded him. "She did totally trash your apartment before she left, and at no time since she left has she contacted you or attempted to apologize for the hundreds of dollars' worth of damage she caused."

Levi looked out toward the lake. "I know." He took a deep breath. "But there was a time not all that long ago when we were close." He turned to look at me again. "At one point I even thought I might have loved her. And it was *me* who broke up with *her*, so maybe she was at least a tiny bit justified in taking a hatchet to my place."

"I don't know about that." I sat quietly in the hot sun as I searched for the right thing to say. I felt the sand from the wooden bench on which we sat dig into my thighs, but I hated to stand up, breaking the intimacy of the moment.

"Either way, I should have met with her and listened to what she wanted to tell me." Levi sighed. "No matter how hard I try to convince myself that anything she might have been involved in leading up to her death were out of my control and therefore not my problem, I can't help feeling like I let her down when she really needed me."

I rested my head against Levi's shoulder in a show of support. His bare skin smelled of coconut and sunshine, most likely from the tanning lotion he'd applied to his already darkening skin. As a physical education teacher and football coach, Levi worked out. A lot. I knew that a good percentage of the dozens of females already lining the waterfront had eyes trained on us, or I guess I should say Levi, as we spoke.

"We *are* going to investigate?" he asked.

I sat up and looked at him. "Do you think we should?"

"I do," Levi decided. "Ellie told me about Barbie's encounter with Salinger on the beach yesterday. I've never really trusted the guy, and now I don't trust him twice as much. If he had something going on with Barbie, he most likely has something to hide, and that something might interfere with his ability to look at all the facts impartially. Besides, Salinger is famous for seeking out the easy and convenient answers and ignoring more complex possibilities. If we leave it up to him, he'll justify his theory that it was an accident and sweep any evidence to the contrary under the rug. I feel like figuring out what really happened and finding Barbie's killer is the least I can do for her."

"So you don't think this was an accident, as Salinger believes?"

"Heck no. You know Barbie. She had many faults, but getting drunk wasn't one of them. She rarely drank. She said alcohol had too many calories. And there's no way she'd risk messing up that dress. She was a fanatic about her wardrobe. The only conclusion I can come to is that someone helped her into the water, and I intend to find out who it was."

I gazed off into the distance as I considered the situation. I'd really hoped to avoid becoming involved in this particular murder investigation. I never had really gotten along with Barbie and I had at least a million other things that I *should* be focusing on at this particular point in my life. I watched a group of men and women set off across the lake on stand-up paddle boards. It would be nice to have some free time to relax and participate in the summertime activities that I loved. I knew that if I agreed to investigate, my free time—all my free time—would be taken up sorting out which of the dozens of people who had motive to kill Barbie actually did. I'd as much as decided to pass on this particular investigation when I turned and looked at Levi. He looked so lost. Like a little boy who'd lost his favorite toy and had no idea where to look.

"Salinger called me while I was at the boathouse getting ready to meet you here," I began. "He said the CSI found Barbie's shoe on the pier. It looked as if it had gotten caught in the space between the boards, causing her to fall forward. Salinger is sticking to the alcohol-impaired theory for now, but he did say that he'd ordered a toxicology screen, so he should have better information later this afternoon."

"Was he planning to call you with the results?" Levi wondered.

"No, but I'm sure Zak can get them."

"So we're going to investigate?" Levi asked again.

"Okay." I took Levi's hand. "I'm in. I'm sure Zak and Ellie will help as well."

"Tonight?" Levi asked.

I thought about the dinner I was supposed to have with my parents, and the adorable stuffed doggie I'd gotten for Harper and couldn't wait to give her. I'd found the doggie in a gift shop in the valley. It was soft and fuzzy and looked almost exactly like Charlie. I hated to miss out on our special night, and this would be the second time I'd had to cancel on my parents, but given the unique set of circumstances, I knew they'd understand.

"Let's meet at the boathouse at six," I said. "We have plenty of beer, wine, and tequila left from last night, and I have left-over steaks we can grill for dinner."

"I'll call Ellie to let her know what we're doing," Levi offered. He grabbed his phone, which was safe in a waterproof case.

"Ask her to bring something for dessert," I requested. "And make it a quick call. It looks like the rest of the water-sports team has arrived and is heading toward the marina. I think I heard someone say we were going to use Nathan's new ski boat. Did you bring your board?"

I realized that he hadn't been carrying it when he'd joined me on the beach.

"It's in my truck."

"I'll get it while you make the call," I volunteered.

"And grab my wet suit while you're at it. It's on the front seat."

"Yeah, okay."

I returned to the parking lot and located Levi's SUV. I was about to head back to the beach with the wakeboard and wet suit when I noticed the dog I'd come to think of as Scamp rummaging through a Dumpster at the edge of the lot. I set Levi's things on his front seat and slowly made my way toward the evasive little dog. I wasn't sure what I was going to do since I didn't have so much as a leash with me, but perhaps if I could lure him back to Levi's vehicle, I could lock him inside and then call Jeremy to come to get him.

"Hey, Scamp," I said in a soothing voice as I slowly made my way forward. Scamp looked up from the takeout containers he was rummaging through when he heard me approach. The dog was filthy, with matted hair and half an ear, but he had intelligent eyes that showed his distrust of me. "I have lots of food back at the Zoo if you want a safe, warm place to hang out for a while."

Scamp tilted his head as if he were actually listening to me. He watched me with interest as I continued to inch forward. "I bet if we give you a bath and a good brushing, we can find you a new forever home with someone who will love you."

I made my way closer to the dog, who looked like he was ready to bolt at any minute. Based on his skittish nature and the condition of his coat, I was willing to bet he'd been on the street for quite some time. I took out my phone and quickly snapped his photo. If he did manage to slip away, at least I could make up flyers to attempt to track him down again. I found myself wishing I had some of the dog treats I normally keep in my pocket.

"What's the holdup?" Levi walked up behind me.

Scamp took one look at the man carrying a wakeboard and took off running.

"I was trying to catch that dog," I answered. "He's been hanging around down here at the beach for a few days. I'm sure he's a stray. I was hoping to coerce him into your vehicle and then have Jeremy come to get him."

"Sorry. The guys sent me to get you. Everyone's here and the boat is loaded."

"Yeah, okay. I'll try to find the dog later."

Chapter 4

I was sorry to miss dinner with my parents and bonding time with my little sis, but it was nice to have just the core group together again. Okay, technically Levi, Ellie, and I are the initial core group, but Zak had always been around on the outskirts of our trio, so when the four of us are together, it somehow feels different than it does when other friends join in. I suspect Ellie specifically didn't invite Rob to attend out of respect to Levi. Rob was a nice-enough guy, and he *was* going to be Ellie's husband, but somehow he hadn't managed to meld with the group the way Zak had.

Zak manned the BBQ while Levi and Ellie chatted and I tried to figure out exactly how to approach the circumstances we faced. Like Levi, I suspected there was more to Barbie's death than Salinger believed. While it was *possible* that Barbie simply got drunk and fell into the water, it was highly unlikely that's what occurred. Barbie was athletic and a good swimmer. If she had fallen in, or even been pushed, it made sense that she could have swum the short distance to shore. And even if she'd had a few drinks, she would have sobered up the minute she hit the cold water of the alpine lake. I suppose if she was extremely drunk or had been taking drugs, she could have passed out and drowned, as Salinger believed.

Levi had been correct in his assumption that the sheriff wasn't going to just hand over the results of the autopsy. Zak promised to see what he could find out after he finished grilling up the most mouthwatering steaks I had eaten in quite some time.

I supposed we should proceed with the assumption that Barbie had been murdered and then focus on defining who might have hated her enough to want to kill her. Unfortunately, I was afraid the list was going to be a long one.

"Do you want another margarita?" Ellie stood in front of me with a pitcher of the frozen drink.

"Sure, why not? How's Levi?" I asked as she poured.

"Kind of a mess," Ellie admitted. Levi had joined Zak at the BBQ, but I could see the concern on her face. "He feels guilty, and I guess I can see why he would. I don't blame him for blowing Barbie off after everything she did, but still . . ."

"Yeah, I know what you mean. I guess the only thing we can do at this point is figure out who did this."

"Barbie wasn't a popular woman," Ellie reminded me. "It might be easier to figure out who *didn't* want her dead."

I looked out toward the lake, where the dogs were chasing each other. Part of me really didn't want to get sucked into another murder investigation, but I did want to help my friend, and solving the murder seemed the best way to do that. I took a sip of my drink. The frozen mixture of lime and tequila was exactly what I needed after the long, hot day. I let myself relax as I waited for the sun to begin its descent behind the mountain.

"I've been thinking about that day at the beach," Ellie said after several minutes of silence. "I hate to admit it, but I pretty much spied on Barbie from the moment she arrived until she left at the end of the day. Chances are someone she came into contact with during the day is either responsible for her death or at least has some knowledge that will help us narrow down who's responsible."

"I guess we can make a list and start talking to people."

Ellie pulled out her phone. "I'll make a list for now, and then we can download it and share it after dinner."

"While I was there, you mentioned Salinger, Lisa and Jason Grover, Conan and his wife or girlfriend, and lifeguard guy," I began.

"There were a few others after you left," Ellie added. "Phillip Hayes stopped to chat with her. At first it seemed like they were just catching up, but then it looked like their conversation turned into an argument. Phillip left shortly after that."

Phillip was one of the men Barbie flirted with when she lived in Ashton Falls. She worked in the local yoga studio, and Phillip delivered bottled water to the studio on a daily basis. I didn't know whether the relationship had progressed beyond flirting, but I did know that Phillip was married. "Okay, let's add Phillip and his wife Angela to the list. Who else?"

"There were several women who used to take yoga from Barbie on the beach that day. Most stopped to say hi, but I doubt it's worth listing them. None seemed angry or put out by her presence."

"What about Serenity?" I asked. Serenity was the owner of the yoga studio and had been very put out when Barbie up and quit without giving any notice.

"Serenity?" Ellie asked. "She seems so . . ."

"Serene. I know. It's her type you usually need to watch out for."

Ellie added her to the list.

"Anyone else?" I wondered.

"Probably, but that's a start. Looks like the steaks are done. Let's eat before they get cold."

Zak was a master at many things, the least of which was grilling the perfect steak. As I sat on the deck that bordered the lake with my friends, I reminded myself of how lucky I was to live in such a beautiful place and to have such wonderful friends to share my life. Although I was beginning to tire of the seemingly endless string of murder investigations I seemed to be drawn into, Levi was my friend, and he'd asked for my help; in spite of my reluctance, I planned to give it to him.

"How did the water-sports meeting go?" Zak asked.

"Really good," Levi answered. "Zoe and I have a killer double routine that's going to knock everyone's socks off."

"Wakeboarding or skiing?" Ellie asked.

"Boarding," Levi answered. "Let's just say that death-defying moves will be involved."

"Death defying?" Zak asked.

"Don't worry, Levi is just being dramatic. Levi and I have been doubling since we were kids. We know what we're doing."

"I hope so," Ellie said. "I'd hate for my maid of honor to have to be pushed down the aisle in a wheelchair."

"Not to worry. I promise to show up free of bruises or broken bones."

"When is this shindig, anyway?" Levi asked.

"We haven't set an *exact* date," Ellie answered. "Maybe July or August."

"One of the men I went sailing with has a house on the beach in Maui," Zak informed us. "He said I could use it any time I'd like, if you and Rob want to honeymoon there."

"Really?" Ellie gasped. "That would be fantastic. I've always wanted to go to Maui but haven't quite managed to get there yet."

"I'm sure Keoke will let you use it, as long as it's available. I'll need a span of dates you plan to be there. Maybe two weeks or so."

"I'll talk to Rob tomorrow."

It bothered me just a bit that Ellie was much more excited about the honeymoon than she was the wedding, and ten times more excited about being a mother than being a wife. It was really nice of Zak to offer the use of his friend's house, but I sort of wish he hadn't. Requiring Rob and Ellie to set a date moved a wedding I wasn't sure should happen all that much closer.

"Are you planning to take Hannah with you on your honeymoon?" I asked.

"I'm sure we will. She's too little to be away from us for so long. She'll love Hawaii."

"The house has three bedroom, four baths, a large living area, and a pool right on the beach," Zak informed Ellie. "I've stayed there and really enjoyed it. It's situated north of most of the touristy spots, so it's quiet yet still close enough to drive to fantastic restaurants."

"It sounds perfect." Ellie hugged Zak. "Thank you so much. I'll talk to Rob tomorrow and nail down a date. Are there any Saturdays that wouldn't work for us to use your house?" Ellie asked Zak.

Zak looked at me.

"I'm pretty open," I responded.

"Yeah, me too," Zak added.

"I'm free as well, if you're interested," Levi added, in a voice that held just a hint of snark.

"Okay, great. I'll check with Kelly and make sure she's free to cover at the Beach Hut and then compare notes with Rob."

"Perhaps we should get back to the murder investigation." Levi seemed annoyed by the wedding talk. "That is, after all, why we're here."

"Ellie and I were talking while you and Zak were grilling," I began. "We have an initial list of possible suspects."

I went over the list and asked for input from Zak and Levi. Zak didn't really know Barbie all that well, but Levi thought we might want to add Courtney Huntington, Barbie's former roommate, and Brock Silvers, the man Barbie had first moved to Ashton Falls for. It occurred to me that although Barbie had only lived in Ashton Falls a short time, she'd managed to make a lot of enemies in what amounted to a handful of months.

"Do we know if there were any defensive wounds that might indicate a struggle?" Ellie asked.

"I might be able to get a peek at the coroner's report," Zak said. "I need access from my desktop. It has a lot better software than the laptop I keep in my truck. Is everyone up for moving this party down the beach to my house?"

"Yeah." I accepted Zak's idea. "I'll clean up here if you want to go ahead and get started. Charlie and I will meet you at your house when I'm finished in the kitchen."

"I'll help you," Ellie offered.

"And I'll go with Zak," Levi decided.

After the guys left, Ellie and I cleared away the remainder of our feast from the table on the deck. Dinner really had been delicious and I was full and lethargic. Part of me just wanted to put on my pj's and curl up with a good book. I owed Levi so many favors, though, and he was one of my two best friends, so I set my own desires aside and packed a few things to take to Zak's should I decide to stay over. I started the dishwasher and then gave Marlow and Spade fresh food and water and cleaned their litter box in case I didn't get back to the boathouse until the following day.

"What do you really think about this whole thing?" Ellie asked as she wiped the countertop.

"Honestly, I'm not sure. Barbie did have a lot of enemies, but unless the coroner's report indicates foul play of some sort, I don't think we have much to go on. It's odd that Barbie called Levi, though."

"You don't think it was just an attempt to secure a date for the evening?"

"Possibly, but sort of doubtful. Barbie and Levi didn't part on good terms. She was a beautiful woman who would have had no problem finding a date. I think there must have been more to the call."

"I hope we can figure this out for Levi's sake. He's really beating himself up over the fact that he didn't agree to meet her."

"Yeah, given what happened, I can see why he might feel guilty. I wonder if Zak's friends are still going to be in town tomorrow."

"Why do you ask?" Ellie wondered.

"The only clothes I have at Zak's are cutoffs, board shorts, flip-flops, and tank tops. It occurred to me that if his friends are still in town, he might want to get together with them. Maybe I should pack a sundress and some nicer sandals."

"I don't suppose it would hurt to keep something nicer at Zak's in any event," Ellie agreed. "Why don't you and Zak just move in together? It would save all this hassle dragging things back and forth."

I sat down on the bed next to Ellie. "I don't think I'm ready for something like that. Besides, I love my boathouse and can't imagine moving, and asking Zak to move in here would be unreasonable."

"Yeah, I see your point. If I lived in this boathouse, I wouldn't want to leave either. It won't be as hard to say good-bye to my little apartment."

"So you're going to move into Rob's house after the wedding?"

"It makes the most sense. Hannah is already settled there, and I'm not sure we can afford something new."

"And it doesn't bother you that Rob lived there with Hannah's mother?" I asked.

Ellie shrugged. "A little. Rob often mentions Cassie in passing. He'll say things like, 'I remember when Cassie picked out that wallpaper,' or 'Cassie had a fit when I brought home that chair.' It would be nice to start fresh in a new place that's just ours."

"Maybe you should talk to Rob about looking for a place. It doesn't seem an unreasonable request from where I sit."

"I did bring up the idea of getting a new place at one point, but Rob said it was silly to go to all the trouble of moving when his house would suit our needs perfectly."

"Yes, but it's his house. It will always *be* his house. I really think you should bring up the subject again. I'm not trying to cause a problem between you, but in the long run I think you'll come to hate his house and all the ghosts that live there."

"Yeah, I get what you're saying. When I first met Rob and he told me that Hannah's mother left shortly after she was born, I got this image in my mind that she wasn't a huge part of Rob's life. But after I began to dig a little deeper into the story, I found out that they lived together for four years before she became pregnant. They only broke up because Cassie didn't want to be a mother at that point in her life, but Rob very much wanted to be a father. Cassie wanted to give Hannah up for adoption and Rob wanted to keep her. If you ask me, in spite of everything that's happened, I think he still has feelings for her."

"Does that concern you?"

"I don't know. Not really. I mean, she's out of the picture. She moved back to Maine, where they both grew up."

"I didn't realize that Rob knew Cassie before moving to Ashton Falls."

"Yeah, they're from the same hometown. They came to Ashton Falls together when she got a job in the area. But like I said, after Hannah was born, she moved back to Maine and Rob stayed here. I don't see her as a threat to our relationship."

I wasn't so sure Ellie had nothing to worry about but didn't say as much. I thought about my mom, who'd put the world as well as twenty-four years between my dad and herself and still found her way back.

Chapter 5

Sunday, May 18

"You think Barbie may have been murdered?" my dad asked the next morning. Zak had invited Dad, Mom, and Harper to brunch to make up for the fact that we'd had to cancel on them the previous evening. I really had wanted to help Levi, but I also felt bad about the frequency with which we seemed to have to postpone our plans with some of the most important people in my life.

"It's possible," Zak confirmed as he passed the fresh fruit salad he'd made to go with the blackberry-covered French toast around the table. He'd set up our feast, which also included both sausage and bacon, on the deck overlooking the lake. This morning, like every morning in paradise, was a perfectly awesome day. "The coroner's report confirmed that Barbie had flunitrazepam, more commonly known by its brand name, Rohypnol, or its street name, roofies, in her system. While the drug could have been ingested voluntarily, it's not unreasonable to suspect that Barbie was slipped the drug without her consent."

"Levi is certain she never would have taken the drug voluntarily," I added as I bit into a piece of cantaloupe. "And I have to say I tend to agree with him on this one. Barbie had many faults, but she was extremely OCD about what she put into her body."

"So someone slipped her the drug and then pushed her off the pier?" Mom speculated.

"Possibly, or she was slipped the drug, became disoriented, and then fell off the pier," Zak offered. "The coroner didn't note any signs of a struggle, and the official cause of death was drowning."

"It's odd that she'd even be on the pier at that time of night," Dad said. "It still gets mighty chilly once the sun goes down."

"Yeah, it is odd," I agreed. "And she didn't have on anything other than a very thin dress when I found her."

"Do you think it's possible she was drugged elsewhere and then dumped into the lake?" Mom asked.

"No. Salinger found a shoe on the pier," I answered. "It appeared Barbie got her heel stuck in the space between the planks of the decking, so she must have been ambulatory at that point."

Harper, who had been sleeping in the portable crib next to us, began to fuss. I pushed away my plate and picked her up. I'd been waiting for her to wake up ever since they'd arrived. I know most of you will think I'm biased, but Harper is the cutest baby in the entire world. I know every new parent or sister thinks that, but trust me, she really is the cutest of the cute.

"I can take her in and change her," Mom offered as I held Harper against my shoulder and rocked her back and forth. I nuzzled my cheek against her head as I took in the smell of her angel-soft hair.

"I'll do it." I picked up the diaper bag, adjusted Harper in my arms, and headed into the house.

Zak had converted one of his extra bedrooms into a nursery, complete with a crib, dresser, and changing table, so Harper would have her own space when we babysat, which we both very much wanted to do. I'd gone just a tiny bit crazy decorating the space in a Noah's Ark theme that featured dozens of stuffed animals arranged on shelves around the room. The walls were painted a pale yellow with white trim, and Ellie had promised to paint a mural of the ark and animals on one of the walls.

I could overhear the conversation on the deck below as I changed Harper's diaper and then dressed her in one of the outfits I'd bought for her. I have to admit I went a little over the top when Zak took me shopping during our trip to New York and I found the most awesome children's store on the planet. I figure Harper has enough clothes to wear each outfit only once, if she's so inclined. After I'd gotten home and unpacked everything I'd had shipped, I realized how completely baby crazy I'd become. Zak suggested we donate some of the clothes to babies in need, which I realized was a worthy and practical idea.

As I stood back to admire how completely adorable my baby sister looked in her yellow duckie dress, I began to understand how Ellie might have gotten so caught up with Hannah as to agree to marry her father just to maintain a relationship that had come to mean so much to her. Harper was my sister and, as such, a permanent part of my life. I tried to imagine how devastated I'd be if Harper was taken away and I was no longer able to see her whenever I wanted. To be honest, I'd worried about that quite a lot when Mom first told me that she was pregnant. My mom isn't known for her staying power, although this time around she seems to have settled down quite nicely. Mom and Dad bought a three-bedroom lakefront house with a converted pool house with the idea that Mom and Harper would live in the former and Dad would live in the latter. It started off that way, but Dad moved into the main house during Mom's final week of pregnancy, and so far it's in the main house where he still resides. Sure, he sleeps in the guest room, but if things go the way I hope, he'll be moving in with Mom officially before too much more time passes.

I looked down on the people I loved most in the world. They'd been discussing Barbie's death, which I'd pretty much tuned out until I heard my dad say, "I don't want Zoe putting herself in danger again."

"Don't worry, I don't want that either," Zak assured Dad. "I'll keep an eye on her."

Like hell. I came so, so close to throwing Harper's wet diaper out of the window and onto the head of my traitor of a boyfriend. He should know by now that if someone was going to keep an eye on Zoe, it was going to be Zoe. I was preparing an angry retort at the very least when Zak looked up toward the window where I was standing and winked. The rat knew I could hear him. I should pummel him for the comment, but I realized that he was just trying to pacify my overprotective father. Have I mentioned what a great boyfriend I have?

"Do you have a plan?" Mom asked.

"Zoe is the brains of the operation," Zak stated with conviction. "I'm simply along to provide any cyberhacking that may be needed, and provide backup where I can."

"She really does seem to have a knack for this detective thing," Dad complimented. "I always knew she was a smart girl."

I grinned as my annoyance turned to pride. I picked up Harper and cradled her in my arms. "We're both smart girls, aren't we, little one?"

Harper smiled, her bright blue eyes staring back at me. I ran a finger over her rosy cheek. I'd never had any siblings before and, although I'd thought about them from time to time, I'd never really longed for them, the way some of the other only kids I knew in school had. And then I met Harper, and I knew that of all the relationships I have had and will have in the future, the bond between sisters is special indeed. I kissed Harper's fuzzy blond head before heading downstairs to return her to Mom for her morning meal.

After breakfast, Mom and Dad headed home. I wanted to have a chat with Salinger, if he happened to be in on a Sunday, while Zak offered to do a cursory background search on each of our suspects to see if anything popped. Levi called me as I drove to the sheriff's office. He told me he had news, so we agreed to meet at Ellie's Beach Hut later that afternoon.

"I figured you might be by today." Salinger showed me into his office.

It seemed like everyone had been saying that to me lately. Was I really that predictable?

"Where's your furry sidekick?" he asked.

"Home with Zak."

"Ah, the felon I'm guessing hacked into my police report. You know I can have him arrested for that?"

"Sure. If you can prove he did it, but you can't, so let's move on, shall we?"

"Fair enough. What can I help you with today?"

I realized that since I had initiated the informal get-together, I'd be in charge of the questions this time around.

"How well did you know Barbie Bennington?" I asked.

Salinger frowned and looked down at his desk. I could tell the question had made him uncomfortable, which is exactly what I'd expected. "I didn't really know the woman at all," he lied.

I waited until Salinger glanced up and then looked him directly in the eye. "And that's the answer you're going to stick with?" I knew that my interrogation method left much to be desired, but I hoped my forthright approach would encourage him to level with me.

Salinger paused. "Are *you* investigating *me*?"

"If you're going to lie to me, I guess I'm going to have to." I hoped I sounded a lot more confident than I felt. The truth of the matter is, Salinger can make my life miserable if he chooses. I know it, and so does he. Challenging him outright probably wasn't my best move, but for some reason I felt that I needed to establish the upper hand if I was going to gain this man's help.

"What makes you think I'm lying?" he asked.

I just smiled. I'd seen a detective do that once in a movie and it had worked spectacularly. I sat in silence, waiting for Salinger to make the next move.

"You don't seriously think I killed the woman?" Salinger spat out.

"I don't know." I paused for affect. "Did you?"

"Of course not."

"But you did know her," I encouraged.

Salinger didn't answer.

"Keep in mind I already know the answer to this question," I prodded.

"Very well," Salinger grunted. "Yes, I knew her. What of it?"

"You had an affair," I stated with a certainty I was far from feeling.

"Now you're just making stuff up." Salinger turned the oddest shade of red, sort of a deep purple with a burgundy finish.

"Am I?" I asked.

I sat quietly and watched the man sitting across from me as he squirmed in his chair. I have to admit I was rather enjoying the show. After all, the guy had put me through it, and it was quite nice to be on the opposite end of the squirm for once.

"I'm not sure you could call what we had an affair," Salinger began tentatively. "I caught Ms. Bennington breaking and entering, and she convinced me that she could make it worth my while to turn a blind eye."

"She convinced you by sleeping with you," I clarified.

"I believe that was implied. I didn't kill her, however, and I'd appreciate it if you'd keep this conversation to yourself. I'd hate for a brief lapse in judgment to ruin everything I've spent my life working for."

"Gee, that would be too bad. I'd hate for a brief lapse in judgment to ruin *anyone's* career." I emphasized the word as a way of reminding him that he'd used my own mistake against me to get me fired from a job I'd loved not all that many months ago.

Salinger looked away. He actually looked guilty. I realized that for the first time in our relationship, I had the power.

"I won't say anything," I assured Salinger. "For now," I qualified. "However, I'll need some things from you."

"Are you blackmailing me?" Salinger tried to appear outraged, but he came off frightened rather than angry.

I smiled. "Yes, I guess I am."

"Oh, very well. What do you want?"

"I'd like to know more about this break-in for starts. Where did Barbie break into? What did she take? When did the break-in occur? Things like that."

"And what, may I ask, do you intend to do with this information?"

As much as I was enjoying my sparring match with Salinger, I really did want to solve Barbie's murder—if there had indeed been a murder—so Levi could put this behind him once and for all. "Look," I said, sitting forward, "I'm not going to rat out your little indiscretion, but I think we should work together on this. We both want to see the issue of Barbie's death resolved one way or the other. You scratch my back and I'll scratch yours. Not literally," I qualified.

"Why is this so important to you?" Salinger wondered.

"Honestly, it's not important to me. I didn't even like the woman. But it's important to Levi, and *he* is important to me."

Salinger sat back in his chair and made a tepee with his fingers. He appeared to be considering my request. I'd seen him make this move many times and knew it was only a matter of time before he agreed to my request.

"You know, you really are turning out to be a pain in the butt," he said.

"Actually, I'm quite famous for it. So do we cooperate?"

"Yeah, okay. On this one case only. Don't get the idea that our partnership is going to be a regular thing."

"God forbid. So about the B&E charge?"

"I was driving home last Wednesday evening when I noticed a light on in the backroom at that antiques shop."

"Trish's Treasures?" I asked.

"No, the shabby little place that's about five miles out of town. I think it's called One Man's Trash."

"Oh, yeah, I know the place you're talking about. Go on."

"I decided to stop to check it out. I found Ms. Bennington preparing to leave through the back door. She had a clock in her hand. The store wasn't open, so I assumed she was stealing it. She begged me not to arrest her. She said she'd seen the clock on a previous visit and fallen in love with it but couldn't afford it, so she decided to steal it. And she made me an offer I couldn't refuse."

I frowned. The entire scenario made no sense. If Salinger had revealed that he'd caught Barbie stealing designer clothes or jewelry, I'd probably buy it, but an old clock from a rundown antiques store that was known for selling more junk than anything else?

"Was there anything special about this clock?" I asked.

Salinger shrugged. "I'm not into antiques, so I couldn't tell you. It was old. The kind you have to wind."

"Did she leave with it?"

"No, I made her leave it behind."

"And she didn't have anything else?" I asked.

"Not that I noticed."

I tried to work the whole thing out in my mind. Something odd was going on, for sure.

"You were seen talking to Barbie at the beach on the day of her death. Do you mind telling me what you were talking about?"

"I don't see that our conversation is any of your business," Salinger pointed out.

"Perhaps not, but I'm curious all the same."

Salinger blushed. "I wanted to see if she was interested in having dinner. At first I thought she was going to accept. She got real close and whispered in my ear. I was expecting her to whisper something dirty, but instead she told me to buzz off. I got angry at her dismissive tone and reminded her that I was keeping her secret. She basically told me that she'd paid her debt and our business was concluded. I got mad and left. I never saw her again until I responded to the drowning call."

"She was with a man in red board shorts. Did you recognize him?"

"No. There was a man, but he got up and headed into the water when I arrived. He didn't say anything and hadn't come back to the beach by the time I left. I suppose he was just her fling of the hour. Now I really need to get back to work, so unless you have anything else for me . . . ?"

"No, that should do it for now." I stood up. "I tell Zak, Levi, and Ellie everything," I emphasized. "But with the exception of the three of them, who won't say anything," I assured him, "your little secret is safe with me."

Chapter 6

After leaving Salinger's office, I headed over to Ellie's Beach Hut. The parking lot was packed as usual, so I parked in the alley behind the shops that lined Main Street. I hadn't wanted to take Charlie with me when I went to visit Salinger, so I'd left him with Zak. If the number of bodies crammed onto the beach and pier were any indication, I was willing to bet that Ellie had done a good amount of business that afternoon. Ellie really did have an awesome setup for those looking to grab a cold drink or quick bite to eat while enjoying the beauty of one of the most popular beaches on the lake. As I ran across the street, dodging traffic in both directions, I noticed a man walking to his truck who looked a lot like the man Ellie and I had referred to as Conan the afternoon we'd been spying on Barbie. He appeared to be alone, so I changed direction and set a trajectory that would cause me to accidentally on purpose run smack dab into the Neanderthal.

"Oh, I'm so sorry," I said as I knocked his keys out of his hand. "I'm such a klutz. I can't believe I ran into you like that. Are you hurt?"

"By a tiny thing like you? Hardly."

"You know, you look familiar. Do we know each other?" I asked, knowing we didn't.

"Perhaps." The man began looking me up and down.

Pervert.

"Aren't you a friend of Barbie's?" I fished.

"You party with Barbie?" The man was practically drooling by now.

"Occasionally. How about you? Are you and Barbie close?"

"We've gotten funky a time or two," the man leered. "Maybe you can call her up and the three of us can get together."

"Yeah, maybe I'll do that. Can I have your number?" I figured if the guy didn't realize Barbie was dead, he couldn't have killed her and most likely didn't know anything at all about what had happened to her, but it couldn't hurt to get his number.

I handed the man a pen and he wrote his number on my hand. Seriously? After he left, I fought the bile that had worked its way into my throat as his sweaty palm caressed mine, and headed toward a table that had just become vacant. I sat down before the party even left, receiving a rude look for doing so, but in this crowd, he who waits, waits.

"Smooth move," Ellie greeted me as she began to clear the table. "Who was that guy you were talking to?"

"Conan."

"Come again?"

"From the beach. That was the guy you referred to as Conan. He was giving me his phone number." I held up my hand.

"You think he knows something about Barbie's death?"

"I don't think he knows much about anything, but I figured it couldn't hurt to have his number just in case. Do you have a piece of paper so I can transfer this from my hand before I soak my arm in battery acid?"

"Battery acid?"

"The guy seemed to think it was necessary to molest my arm while he jotted down his number. I almost vomited on his shoe."

Ellie laughed. "Well, I should think so. We have some pretty strong soap in the back. It's not battery acid strong, but it should do the trick. Go ahead and wash up. I'll save your table."

By the time I'd washed Conan's grubby paw prints off my hand and arm, Levi had shown up. We both ordered a beer while we waited for Zak to arrive and Ellie to get caught up enough to take a break. The cold beer on a hot day went a long way toward settling my queasy stomach. There's something about sitting by the water on a warm afternoon that makes life's little disturbances seem inconsequential at best. I found myself wishing I'd taken the time to go back to the house to get Charlie. He'd love sitting in the shade next to me, watching the kids on the beach chase each other along the waterline. I was lucky to have a dog who was so easygoing with any person and in any situation. Ellie sat down next to Levi at about the same time I saw Zak jogging down the beach with my furry bundle of joy. Charlie trotted over to me as Zak took a quick dip in the lake to cool off before joining us.

"I want you to taste a new appetizer I'm thinking about offering." Ellie set a bowl of dip on the table in front of us. "Be honest about whether you like it. When I first came up with the concept, it seemed like it would be delicious, but I've tried a couple of different versions and it doesn't seem quite right."

I picked up one of the tortilla chips she'd brought to accompany the dip and took a bite. It was good. Really good. "I like it," I commented.

"Yeah, but I can see what Ellie means." Levi took a second bite. "Maybe if you add some hot pepper sauce. It's good, but a little pepper sauce would give it more of a kick."

Ellie took a bite and thought about it. "Or maybe horseradish. It would give it a kick and provide an interesting flavor. Thanks, Levi."

"Always happy to help a damsel in distress."

Zak came over to the table and sat down next to me. Ellie offered him a beer, but he declined.

"You jogged all the way from your house?"

Zak nodded to me. "I needed to get some exercise, and I figured Charlie and I could get a ride home with you." Zak took a bite of the dip. "Hey, this is really good. New menu item?"

"Maybe, if I can get it just right," Ellie answered.

"You didn't bring Lambda?" I asked Zak about his dog.

"No. He's been limping again, and I didn't want to put too much stress on his joints. I have an appointment to take him in to see Scott this week. I'm afraid his arthritis might be getting worse. It seems like he's in pain a lot of the time lately."

"Poor baby. Maybe Scott can change his meds." Lambda had been involved in a run-in with a black bear and was near death when I found him almost five years earlier. I'd brought him to the shelter and, with Scott's expert doctoring, we'd nursed him back to health. Lambda was a young dog at the time of the attack and healed quickly, but his altercation left him with some permanent disabilities, and I worried about his ability to age gracefully.

"Maybe. It seems like he's having a hard time getting around, but hopefully he'll be okay as long as we keep him quiet for a day or two," Zak answered.

"Did you find out anything new about Barbie's murder?" Levi asked Zak. It was obvious he felt the death of a friend trumped doggie ailments when it came to picking a topic of conversation.

"Not really. It seems Barbie had been totally off the grid. I couldn't find any record of her at all since she left Ashton Falls three months ago, which in and of itself is strange."

"Why so?" Ellie asked.

"If she applied for a job or rented an apartment or changed the address on her credit cards, I would have found it. The fact that I didn't find *anything* makes it look like she was hiding out. I looked at the address she has on file at the post office. She closed her box before she left but didn't leave a forwarding address. I talked to the woman who works in the back, and she said any mail for her that came their way was sent back to the sender as undeliverable. She let it slip that Barbie actually had quite a bit of mail sent back, including a tax return. It seems odd that she wouldn't leave a forwarding address if she were expecting a check."

"It's like she just dropped off the face of the earth," Ellie stated.

"Yeah, she did seem to have disappeared," Levi agreed. "I asked around, and no one had heard from her at all until she called me on Thursday."

"She was here on Wednesday," I supplied. I filled the gang in on my conversation with Salinger.

"Why in the world would Barbie steal a clock from that shabby antiques store?" Levi questioned. "I tried to get her to look through a used bookstore once, and she asked me why I would want to buy a book that someone else had owned already. Barbie wasn't the type to appreciate anything old or worn."

"Maybe it was valuable?" Ellie speculated.

"If Barbie wanted valuable, she would have gone for jewelry. Or shoes," Levi added. "Barbie loved shoes."

"Yeah, it doesn't track that Barbie would have been in that shop in the first place to notice the clock," I agreed with Levi.

"Maybe Salinger was lying," Ellie suggested.

"About which part?" Levi asked.

"All of it. Maybe he didn't find Barbie in that particular shop holding a clock."

"The man admitted to letting a thief go in exchange for sexual favors. Why would he lie about something as inconsequential as the *what* and *where*?" I asked.

Ellie shrugged. "I don't know. It's just that the whole thing doesn't fit what we know to be true about Barbie."

Ellie had a point. The fact that Barbie would break into a dusty antiques store and attempt to steal a clock didn't make sense. I'd been in the store in question a time or two, and I was fairly certain the man who owned the establishment dealt more in junk than in treasure. The only possible scenario that made sense was that Barbie was stealing the clock for someone else. The question was, who? If she'd been off the grid, she must have been living with someone for the past three months. Maybe if we found out who she'd shacked up with, we'd find out who killed her.

"Have we learned anything else?" Levi asked. He was obviously becoming agitated.

"I'm pretty sure Conan didn't do it. He didn't seem to know that Barbie was dead," I added.

"Conan? As in the guy on the beach?"

"Yeah. I ran into him on my way over," I informed Levi.

"I talked to Angela Hayes today," Ellie contributed. "She wasn't unhappy to hear that Barbie was dead, but it didn't seem like she was responsible for the act either. She mentioned that she and Phillip went sailing with a friend and then headed to the Wharf for dinner. You can check with the staff at the restaurant, but I'd be willing to bet she was telling the truth."

"Yeah, but if Barbie died at between eleven and one, they could have gone to dinner and still had enough time to return to the pier and kill her," Levi pointed out.

"Maybe. But it seems unlikely," Ellie defended herself.

I had to agree with Ellie; it did seem unlikely. I glanced at Charlie, who had crawled under the table and fallen asleep on my foot. The feel of his furry head against my bare foot gave me a feeling of contentment that I can't quite describe. I didn't want to say as much to Zak, but I was worried about his large chocolate lab. If the arthritis we'd been battling got much worse . . . well, I didn't want to think about it.

"I'm going to go to the yoga studio in the morning to talk to Serenity." I jumped back into the conversation as a way to divert attention from my uneasy thoughts.

"You'd better go prepared to take a class," Ellie said. "The watchdog at the desk doesn't let anyone in unless they're supposed to be there."

"Maybe you can get the scoop on Barbie and Phillip while you're there," Levi suggested. "The guy gives me the creeps, and I agree with you that he had plenty of time to kill Barbie after he finished his dinner. He could have eaten, taken his wife home, and then gone back and killed Barbie."

"Honestly, now that I think about it, it seems unlikely, but I'll see what I can find out," I promised.

"I can get in contact with Courtney," Ellie offered. "Her boutique is just down the street. I'll find a few minutes to get away."

"I have classes all day tomorrow and then baseball practice after school," Levi informed us. "I doubt I'll have time to do much of anything, but if I get the opportunity to talk to anyone on our list, I'll take it. How about we all meet tomorrow night and share what we find out?"

"Sounds good. Oh wait." I grimaced. "*American Sensation* is on tomorrow night. We'll have to meet on Tuesday."

"*American Sensation*?" Levi asked. "That show with the singers?"

"That'd be the one," I confirmed.

"You're seriously sitting here telling me that watching a show called *American Sensation* is more important than finding Barbie's killer?"

"Well, it's not *more* important," I conceded, "but it *is* the final episode of the season. By ten o'clock tomorrow night, everyone will know who's going to be America's next sensation."

"Can't you record it?" Levi wondered.

I shook my head in the negative. "I did that last year and it was a total horror show. I overslept and wasn't able to watch it before I went to work, so I spent the entire day warning everyone I saw that they'd die a slow and painful death if they let slip the results. And that wasn't even the worst part. I was terrified that I'd overhear the results on the radio or as part of a television update or Internet story, so I had to avoid all contact with everything electronic for the entire day. It was literally the most stressful day of my life."

Levi looked at me like I'd lost my mind. "You've been almost killed more than once and missing the final episode of *American Sensation* was *literally*," he drew out the word, "the most stressful day of your life?"

"Don't judge," I insisted. "The show is addicting."

Levi looked at Zak.

"It *is* addicting," Zak, fantastic boyfriend that he is, totally backed me up.

"How about we meet for breakfast on Tuesday?" I suggested.

"I have to be at work at eight," Levi reminded me.

"So we can meet at seven. Rosie's is close to the high school. We can compare notes and you can still be at work on time."

"Or," Ellie offered, I assume in an attempt to keep Levi from totally flipping out, "we could meet before *American Sensation*. The show doesn't start until eight. I'm off at six, and everyone else is off before that. We can have dinner at the boathouse. I'll bring food from Ellie's and we can talk before the show airs."

"Works for me," I said. "As long as everyone is quiet during the broadcast."

"Yeah, okay. Works for me too," Levi agreed.

Chapter 7

Monday, May 19

The next morning I called Jeremy and told him that I'd be in late. Then I headed over to Serenity's yoga studio. I was glad I'd taken Ellie's advice and come prepared to take a class; the woman at the desk was a piranha. A teeny, tiny piranha who probably weighed less than I did but had a way about her that made you take a step back when she glared at you. After being informed that Serenity wasn't to be disturbed by anyone not attending a class, I forked over forty bucks—yes, I said forty bucks—and headed toward the locker room. I changed into a tank top and yoga pants and then went down the hall to the room where the class was to be held. By the time I arrived, it was mostly full, so I laid out my mat in the back, near the door.

Serenity came into the room in a cloud of smoke. I hoped for a moment that the place was on fire and we'd all be required to leave, but then I noticed the sticks of incense. Serenity greeted the group and began a routine that thankfully began with what seemed to be nothing more than a series of easy poses focusing on warming up and stretching out our muscles. Unfortunately, I'd signed up for an advanced class, and easy poses segued to impossible contortions in a matter of minutes.

I transitioned from something called Cobra and was preparing to slide into Downward Dog when I felt the muscles in the back of my legs begin to tremble. By the time we worked our way through several other positions and back around to Pigeon Pose, I thought I was going to die. Things went downhill from there. Please understand, I'm in good shape. I run and participate in many athletic activities. The fact that everyone else in the room seemed to be able to twist themselves into a pretzel with no problem while I could barely handle basic, beginner poses was sobering indeed.

By the time Serenity instructed the class to rest in Child's Pose, I was pretty sure I was going to vomit. Luckily, I hadn't eaten breakfast. Once the class was released, I gathered my mat and followed Serenity down the hall and into her office. I collapsed in one of the chairs provided for visitors.

"Water."

Serenity offered me a bottle, which I gratefully accepted. I drank half of it in one long gulp. Serenity was tall and lean, with graceful limbs and long blond hair she'd braided down her back. Next to her, I felt like a duck in a pond full of swans.

"I didn't realized you were interested in yoga," Serenity began when I came up for air.

"Oh, yeah," I gasped. "I do it all the time. Big, big fan."

"I see." The doubt on her face was evident. "What can I help you with?"

"Actually, I wanted to ask you about Barbie."

"What about Barbie?"

"I guess you heard she drowned."

"Yes." Serenity paused. I noticed a small tear forming in the corner of her eye. She looked up toward the ceiling, I assumed in an attempt to get her emotions under control, and not to check for cobwebs. She took a deep breath, closed her eyes, and then lowered her head and looked at me. "I'm sorry. I guess I'm having a harder time with this than I realized."

"I know the two of you were close before she left."

"Barbie and I were never really all that close, but we did share a common passion. I enjoyed our time together at the studio."

"I guess you must have been pretty mad when she left so abruptly."

"Mad?" Serenity stared at me. "I wouldn't say I was mad. I was sad that she chose to leave, but I understood why. Barbie had a certain reputation with men. Most thought her somewhat heartless. And perhaps she was. But there's one thing I know for certain, and that is that she loved your friend. She was devastated when he broke things off."

"Really?" I have to admit I wasn't expecting that.

Serenity drew her legs up onto the chair she was sitting on and folded them under her thin body. "Barbie had a way about her that was off-putting to most women, but I can assure you she had the capacity for deep emotional bonds."

"Did you stay in contact with her after she left town?"

"For a while," Serenity answered. She tucked a stray lock of long blond hair behind her ear before she went on. "I noticed a change in her after she'd been away several weeks. I hated to cut off ties with her, but after much consideration, I accepted that her energy was no longer a complement to my own."

"What kind of a change?" I asked.

Serenity leaned back and closed her eyes. She looked so comfortable, despite the fact that her legs were still folded in an impossible fashion. For a moment I thought she'd gone to sleep, and then she began to speak. "Barbie never had been one to overshare, but I noticed that the longer she was away, the more guarded and secretive she became. She'd never been very good at lying—she was the type to tell things like they were, even if her comments hurt someone else's feelings—and yet I could tell she was lying about many of the things we discussed. I never knew why exactly, but I assumed it had to do with the fact that she'd begun spending time with people who brought negative energy into her world."

"Did she say anything specific about those people?" I asked.

Serenity shrugged. "Not really. She mentioned that her friends had an idea that would make them all a lot of money, and perhaps when she got her share, she'd open a studio of her own. Her disinclination to offer specifics, as well as the guarded tone in her voice, led me to believe that whatever it was she was into wasn't entirely legal. I cut off contact with her shortly after that."

"Did she mention anything about antiques?"

"Antiques?" Serenity frowned. "No, I can't say that she did. Why do you ask?"

"No reason. I'm just trying to pull together some random pieces of information I've come across. Although Levi broke up with Barbie and apparently broke her heart, he did care for her. I'm trying to help figure out who might have wanted to hurt her. Can you think of anything that might help us narrow things down?"

Serenity stared out of the window as she appeared to be considering my question. It was a beautiful day, but as I watched the second hand on the old wall clock begin its fourth revolution, the silence between us made me want to jump out of my chair. Serenity, on the other hand, seemed quite content to sit quietly as the minutes ticked away. I suppose the ability to sit in complete silence and feel comfort in that silence is something that speaks of emotional control and being in the moment. I, on the other hand, have never been known for my emotional control.

"There is one thing," she finally said. "Barbie mentioned that she'd met a man. She said he was a total babe and they had a lot of fun together, but I got a weird vibe."

"Weird how?"

"I don't know. Just weird."

"Do you remember a name?"

"No," Serenity answered. "I'm pretty sure Barbie never mentioned it."

"And do you remember when you had this conversation?"

"I guess about two months ago."

"Okay; thank you for your time." I got up to leave and started toward the door. "Oh, by the way . . ." I turned. "What can you tell me about Barbie's relationship with Phillip Hayes?"

Serenity laughed. "I'd say that any relationship that existed between Barbie and Phillip is wishful thinking on Phillip's part. Barbie had a type and he isn't it."

"I'd heard rumors."

"Most likely started by Phillip. Trust me, there was nothing going on between the two, other than a little harmless flirting when Phillip delivered the water. Barbie had this way about her. She used to love to get guys worked up and then shut them down. In my opinion, it was cruel, but I guess most guys realized Barbie was out of their league and let it go."

After I showered and changed into my street clothes, I headed home to pick up Charlie before going to the Zoo. Now that Jeremy had Morgan to care for and I'd started to travel more often with Zak, we'd turned more responsibility over to our new full-time employee, twenty-three-year-old Tiffany Middleton. Tiffany was mature, energetic, friendly, and quickly becoming a favorite among the town's residents.

"Hey, Tiff," I greeted her as Charlie and I strolled in through the front door. "Jeremy around?"

"He responded to an aggressive-dog call. He should be back anytime. How was your yoga class?"

"Torture."

Tiffany laughed. "Serenity can be tough. I've taken a few of her classes. I could barely walk after the first one."

"Tell me about it. I seriously doubted my ability to get up off the floor after the class was finished. Did the family who applied to adopt Shep show up?"

"Yeah, they came in first thing. I think they'll be a good match. Shep is such a mellow dog, and they have two small children to consider. They said they might know of a family for Polly as well." Tiffany's brown eyes lit up as she spoke.

"I hope it's not a family with small kids." Polly was a very active lab who was sweet but needed a living situation where she could expend some of her energy in a constructive way.

"No, they said they had in mind a middle-aged couple who are suffering from empty nest syndrome now that their youngest has gone off to college. The man is a runner and the woman likes to mountain bike."

"Sounds promising."

"They took an application with them and planned to speak to the couple within the next few days. Oh, by the way, Jeremy told me to let you know that the four dogs we're expecting from Bryton Lake should be here later this afternoon."

"Do we have pens ready?" I glanced toward the hallway that led to the domestic animal cages.

"Bobby got them ready yesterday."

"It seems like Bobby is really working out. He has a knack for anticipating what needs to be done before we even ask him to do it."

"Yeah, Bobby is great," Tiffany agreed. "Did he tell you that his parents are going to match what he saves toward a new car? He thinks he might be able to afford something by the end of the month."

"That's awesome. I bet he's really excited. Has he started looking around yet?"

"Yeah. Most of the cars he's interested in are out of his price range, but I'm sure he'll find something just for getting around."

"I remember my first car." I thought back to that wonderful moment nine years ago when I laid down my hard-earned cash and bought a beat-up old Mustang. "It was a total clunker, but I was so excited to have my own wheels. Of course, it broke down more often than it ran, but it was mine and I loved it."

"My first car was a huge, four-door sedan my grandparents gave me when they got a new car," Tiffany shared. "I could never afford to drive it since it only got around five miles to the gallon, but it looked good sitting in front of the house. When I looked for the car I have now, I decided to get an economy model that gets good mileage."

I laughed. "My Mustang wasn't all that big, but it did seem to guzzle a lot of gas. I, however, didn't learn my lesson in terms of expense; my truck gets even fewer miles to the gallon."

"Yeah, but it's perfect for doing what you do. If we were dependent on my little car, we'd never have been able to transport Goliath yesterday."

"True. Did Gunner say how he did last night?" Goliath is a mountain lion that was found by hikers. He'd been shot and was in bad shape, but Scott Walden seemed to think he'd recover. Thanks to my four-wheel drive and high ground clearance, I was able to drive off-road to the spot where the forest service had tracked him down and tranquilized him.

"Gunner left before I got here," Tiffany informed me. "I checked on him this morning and he seems to be doing better. I talked to Scott yesterday and he thinks he'll make a full recovery."

"Yeah, I talked to Scott as well. He really is a beautiful animal."

"Scott's a really good vet," Tiffany observed.

"Yeah, he knows his stuff."

"Do you know if he's involved?" Tiffany asked.

"Involved?"

"With a woman. Does he have a wife or a girlfriend?"

"Not that I know of. You interested?"

Tiffany blushed. "Maybe. We seem to have a lot in common."

"So ask him out," I suggested.

"You think I should?" Tiffany seemed uncertain.

I shrugged. "Sure, why not? The worst that can happen is that he'll say no. Keep it light. Suggest a movie, or maybe dinner."

"Okay, maybe I will."

I stopped into my office to check my messages and then headed down the hall, where I ran into Jeremy.

"It looks like we have ourselves a biter." Jeremy was leading a lab mix on a leash.

"Oh, no. What happened?" I asked. Once a dog starts biting, it's often difficult to get it to stop.

"Scooter Sherwood."

I groaned. Scooter was a nine-year-old tornado who tended to blow through town, destroying everything in his path. Saying that Scooter was undisciplined didn't do justice to how huge a disaster the boy really was. I honestly don't know why the child hadn't been taken from his drunk of a father years ago, but apparently as long as a parent required their child to attend school, gave them food and shelter, and didn't beat them, they were deemed fit.

"Scooter decided it would be a good idea to pounce on Sally Brown while she was walking Cody, and Cody bit him," Jeremy explained. "I wasn't going to bring him in, but Scooter's dad showed up and insisted on it."

"He wouldn't go for a home quarantine?" I asked.

"Nope. Said he was gonna petition to have the dog destroyed." Jeremy escorted Cody into an empty cage.

"That's ridiculous."

"Yeah. Sally is beside herself, but there isn't much I can do until this gets straightened out."

I pulled the door to the pen closed after Jeremy exited. I felt bad for the poor dog, who was just trying to protect the little girl he loved. "Has Cody bitten anyone before?" I asked.

"He bit Scooter once before," Jeremy informed me. "I guess Sally's dad slipped Scooter's dad some money, and the incident was never reported to us or the sheriff, but Scooter's dad brought it up today, and Sally's mom didn't deny his allegation."

I frowned. "That's bad."

"Yeah, it's not looking good for Cody."

"I'll have a chat with both Scooter's dad and Sally's parents," I offered. "Maybe I can mediate an agreement of some sort."

"Good luck." Jeremy headed back down the hall. "Scooter's dad was pretty mad."

"Yeah, it's going to be tough to get the guy to be reasonable," I agreed as I followed Jeremy. "Still, if I were a dog, I'd want to bite Scooter."

"Right there with you." Jeremy laughed. "While I was at the scene talking to everyone, Scooter went next door to the market and dumped a display cart of tomatoes onto the floor. Ernie was pretty mad, but Scooter said he didn't see the cart and accidently ran into it with his skateboard."

"Seems like stuff like that happens a lot. Maybe we can use the fact that Scooter attacked Sally as a defense for poor Cody."

Jeremy ran a hand through his long bangs. "Couldn't hurt to bring it up, but a good attorney will argue that a dog who bites is a dog who bites. Best we can hope for is to get Scooter's dad to drop the whole thing before attorneys get involved."

"Maybe I'll leave a little early and stop by to talk to Scooter's dad," I offered.

"I wouldn't bother. The guy was toasted. Maybe you can get him to see reason after he sobers up."

"I'll stop by his place in the morning."

Chapter 8

By the time I got back to the boathouse, both Levi and Ellie were already there. Ellie had brought bruschetta, crab-stuffed mushrooms, and salmon wheels for appetizers, which she was arranging on a platter, while Zak was busy cutting up veggies for steak kabobs. After greeting everyone, I hurried upstairs to slip into a pair of shorts and a tank top. One of the things I love best about the advent of warmer weather is the ability to dress down when I get home rather than having to pile on the layers.

The first thing I noticed after I climbed the stair to the loft I use as a bedroom was that the dirty laundry had been removed from the hamper and scattered across the floor. "Marlow," I called. The fuzzy orange ball of fur in question jumped into my arms from atop the dresser. "What in the heck have you been doing all day?" Marlow began to purr. I set him on the bed and began gathering up my clothes while the mischievous cat watched me. Spade, who had been sleeping in my reading chair in front of the window when I came in, is a quiet cat who rarely if ever gets into trouble, but if Marlow can find something to get into, you'd better bet he was going to do so.

I took off my jeans and put on a pair of cut-off shorts. Marlow rolled over onto his back and began to purr. I tossed my jeans in the hamper and then scratched his belly before I pulled my hair into a long ponytail and replaced the tennis shoes I'd worn to work with bright yellow flip-flops. I secured the lid of my hamper after cleaning up Marlow's mess, picked up the loveable bundle of fur, and headed back downstairs.

"Have an appetizer." Ellie pushed a plate in front of me.

I picked up a piece of freshly baked sourdough bread covered with a colorful blend of olives, tomatoes, shrimp, and onion and took a bite. "Um, this is really good."

"Thanks; it's a new blend I'm experimenting with for my summer menu. Try the salmon wheels. I'd like to add a few entries to the menu that are lighter than the standard chicken wings and stuffed mushrooms."

"Oh, I don't know. I like the wings," Levi commented. "My favorite are the nitro wings with a beer." He walked over to the refrigerator to retrieve the aforementioned beverage.

"Try a glass of chardonnay with a mushroom." Ellie handed me a glass of the chilled wine.

"Thanks. It's been a long day." I explained about both my unpleasant experience at Serenity's yoga studio and the dilemma with Cody.

"That Scooter is something else," Ellie agreed. "He was skateboarding on the pier the other day and accidently knocked over two of my trashcans, which were almost filled to the top. It was a huge mess that took me almost an hour to clean up. When I tried to talk to him about respecting other peoples' property, he called me a four-letter word and kicked over one of the benches before leaving."

"Kid sounds angry," Zak observed.

"Yeah, he does take out his aggression on everyone and everything," Levi said. "I heard he got kicked out of school and his dad is homeschooling him, but I don't think there's much schooling going on. The guy went off the deep end when his wife died. It's really a sad situation."

"Kicked out of school?" I questioned. "Scooter blows through town every day just prior to school starting and then again soon after it's over. I just assumed he was going to and from."

"As far as I know, he got kicked out over two months ago. Must not have wanted the fact that he didn't need to make the trip interfere with his regularly scheduled vandalism."

"I'm not busy tomorrow if you want me to stop by to talk to Scooter's dad on Cody's behalf," Zak volunteered.

"He might be more apt to listen to you," I responded.

"Okay, let me take a shot and we'll see what happens."

"So how did your conversation with Serenity go?" Levi asked.

I filled the group in on everything I'd learned, including the fact that Serenity had maintained a relationship with Barbie after she left town until she began lying and acting strangely. I also filled them in on Barbie's relationship with some new guy, and the fact that she was thinking of breaking things off with him. I didn't mention the depth of Barbie's feelings for Levi but did wind things up with the fact that Serenity didn't think Phillip Hayes had actually had an affair with our victim.

"Sounds like this new guy could be a suspect," Ellie commented.

"I think we should add him to the list," I agreed.

"I'd keep Phillip on the list as well," Zak said. "Just because Barbie didn't return his affections doesn't mean he wasn't obsessed with her. She had a way of getting a man's attention."

Zak winked at me to let me know I shouldn't feel threatened by the comment and surprisingly, I didn't. "I'll see if I can track Phillip down tomorrow."

"I spoke to Courtney today," Ellie added. "She didn't say anything that would cause me to believe she killed Barbie, but she did seem to be hiding something. I don't think we should take her off the list just yet."

"I know you said you wouldn't be doing any investigating today." I turned to Levi.

"True, but I did have time to go to the post office."

"And?" I prodded. There had to be more to his statement than that.

"There was an envelope in my box. It didn't have a return address, but I recognized Barbie's handwriting."

"She sent you a letter?" I asked.

"She sent me this." Levi set a newspaper on the counter.

"Why would she send you a newspaper?" I asked.

"I think it's a clue," Levi provided.

"What kind of clue?"

"Barbie and I watched a movie a while back in which spies from two different countries communicated by placing an ad in the classified section of a specific newspaper. To most people the ad would look like any other, but to the men involved, it was really a code. We laughed about it and joked that if we ever went into spying, we'd do the same thing. This is the weekend edition of the *Bryton Lake Courier*. It came out on Friday morning. I called the paper and was told that there were seven new ads placed on Thursday for the weekend edition. My theory is that after I blew Barbie off, she took out the ad, picked up the paper on Friday, and mailed it to me."

"Do you know which ad was the one she took out?" I asked.

"No. The guy I spoke to at the paper said no one by the name of Barbie Bennington took out an ad. She must have used a fake name."

"Did you read the ads?" Ellie asked. "Maybe you can figure it out."

"Of course I read the ads," Levi snapped.

Ellie appeared to be stricken by the tone of Levi's voice.

"Let's all look at them and see if we notice anything," I said.

"How about we eat first?" Zak suggested. "The veggies are chopped, the steak is marinated, and the grill is fired up and ready to go. What do you say we move this party out onto the deck?"

"Sounds good. It really is a beautiful evening. Can you believe this weather?" I was trying for casual conversation as a way to diffuse the tension between Levi and Ellie. "I heard we're in for record high temperatures in the next week or so. I'm predicting a busy holiday weekend."

"It beats that Memorial Day when we got two feet of snow," Zak agreed.

"It's been busier than I anticipated for this time of year at the Beach Hut," Ellie added. "I'm thinking about adding evening hours if I can find enough staff to handle them. These kabobs look wonderful and would be an easy addition if I decide to do a dinner menu. I could offer steak, shrimp, chicken, all veggie."

"You could even offer an all-meat/no-garden option for us carnivores," Levi suggested.

"Well, these are done," Zak announced. "Everyone grab a drink and some salad and let's eat before they get cold."

After dinner we looked at the seven new ads and tore them apart. Two of them were for cars for sale, one of which might be perfect for Bobby. Two others were help-wanted ads, one for a hairdresser and one for a delivery driver. There was an ad announcing an estate auction and another listing an antique cabinet for sale, and the final ad was for an apartment for rent. None stood out as odd or suspicious. If Barbie was trying to communicate through one of the ads, she might have done too good a job hiding the message.

"Could there be another reason Barbie sent you this newspaper?" Ellie asked.

"Like what?"

"I don't know. Maybe there's something significant about one of the articles, or there's an ad in the main body that warrants our attention. If she placed a clue in the classifieds, I'm not seeing an obvious message."

"Here's our ad for the Memorial Day event," I pointed out. "You did a nice job designing it," I complimented Ellie.

"Thanks. Levi is mentioned as a participant and organizer for the event; maybe Barbie saw the ad and wanted you to know she was thinking about you."

"I doubt Barbie would bother with something like that," Levi pointed out. "I'm sure her purpose in sending me the paper relates back to her. Maybe I'll sleep on it to see if anything comes to me during the night."

"Might be a good idea," I agreed. "Right now I'm headed in to watch *American Sensation.* Anyone want to watch it with me?"

"I will," Ellie offered.

"I'll be in after I clean up out here," Zak said.

"I think I'll head home. Thanks for dinner." Levi got up and dusted the sand from his shorts. "I'll see everyone tomorrow."

Charlie climbed up into my lap as I sat down next to Ellie, who was holding Marlow. Once the sun went down, the temperature had begun to drop sharply, so I lit a fire and put on a pot of coffee before turning on the television and settling in for two hours of competition madness. Like most everyone in the country, I had a singer I was rooting for. The suspense of finding out whether he'd win was almost more than I could bear.

"Do you think Levi will be okay?" Ellie asked after he left.

"I'm not sure," I responded as I waited for the commercial break to wrap up. "He's really taking this hard. I think it would be difficult for him in any event, but with the added stress of receiving the phone call from Barbie, it's like the whole thing is doing a number on him."

"I'm really worried about him. He's taking this investigation seriously. I can't believe he didn't want to stay to see Tina win the crown."

"Tina? Are you kidding me? Tim is the obvious choice."

"Oh, I don't know," Ellie countered. "Tina has a lot more people appeal."

"But Tim has a better voice," I argued.

Ellie shrugged. "Sure, if you like that kind of thing. He's a bit edgy for my taste."

"Edgy? What do you mean *edgy*? Just 'cause he has his own style doesn't mean he's edgy."

"I just prefer Tina's mainstream appeal. She really is a little bit country and a little bit rock and roll."

"So you're saying she's indecisive."

"No, I'm not saying that at all. I just think she's a bit more versatile than the others."

I rolled my eyes. I couldn't believe Ellie didn't see that Tim was the clear choice for the crown. "Shhh," I instructed. "They're about to start."

Zak came in from the deck and sat on the other side of me. Spade crawled into his lap, while Lambda laid at his feet. It was nice that there were as many laps as animals this evening. "So what do you think?" Zak asked as he settled in. "Carmen all the way?"

Chapter 9

Tuesday, May 20

The next morning I did what I did every Tuesday morning, headed to Rosie's to meet with the Events Committee. I learned a long time ago that if you missed a meeting, you were going to be nominated to do something no one else wanted to do. There are currently eight committee members. Willa Walton works for the county and serves as the committee chair and county liaison. The money that's earned as a result of the events the committee sponsors technically belongs to the county, and it's Willa's job to be sure that those deserving of the funds end up with them. In addition to Willa, my dad, Hank Donovan, is a volunteer for the fire department, Hazel Hampton represents the library, Tawny Upton attends on behalf of the subsidized preschool she runs, and Levi is the representative for the afterschool sports program, while Ellie uses the funds she helps to earn for an afterschool dance program. Gilda Reynolds is in charge of the community arts project, and I represent animal control and welfare. We'd lost Frank Valdez when he was arrested for attempting to rob the bank the previous month.

On this particular Tuesday morning, Levi was the only member not in attendance. Willa shared that he was sick and had taken the rest of the week off from his job as a high-school gym teacher and coach. She questioned whether he'd be able to fulfill his commitment to the water-sports team and I volunteered to check with him and let them know. After a brief discussion, it was confirmed that everyone in attendance had followed through with the tasks assigned to them and we were in good shape for the upcoming Memorial Day weekend.

After the meeting, Ellie walked me out to my truck, which I had parallel parked on the street in front of the restaurant prior to the meeting. "Do you think Levi is really sick?" she asked.

"He seemed fine last night. My gut tells me that he's upset about everything that's happened and decided he needed some time off."

"He did seem to be working with a short fuse last night," Ellie admitted.

"He feels responsible for Barbie's death. Whether he could have done anything to help her or not, I'm sure it's difficult to live with the knowledge that he didn't even try."

"I'm really worried about him," Ellie repeated what she'd said the night before.

"Yeah, me too."

"Maybe I'll take him some food later and check in on him."

"That could be a good idea. I think I'm going to try to track down Phillip," I said. "I know it's a long shot, but the faster we solve this thing, the faster Levi can get on with his life."

"You think he knows anything?" Ellie asked.

I shrugged. "Probably not. His wife did provide a good alibi, but I still keep thinking about the timeline between his having dinner and Barbie's death. If we can find out what he did after dinner, we can cross him off of our suspect list."

"I've been thinking about my conversation with Courtney," Ellie shared. "She claimed she hadn't spoken to Barbie in ages and had no idea what she might have been up to prior to her death, but I had the overall impression that she wasn't telling me everything. I couldn't quite put my finger on what it was that was bothering me, but I woke up in the middle of the night and it dawned on me that there was a photo of Barbie and Courtney on the wall behind the counter in her boutique."

"So? They were friends and roommates. Why wouldn't Courtney have a photo of the two of them?"

"Yeah, but Courtney said she hadn't seen Barbie for ages. When we saw Barbie at the beach last Friday, do you remember anything different about her?"

I thought about it. "Her hair. She'd cut her hair since she left in February."

"Exactly, and the photo I saw in the boutique featured Barbie with her new hairdo."

"So Courtney must have spent time with Barbie sometime in the past three months," I realized.

"I'd say within the past month. They were on the beach and the snow was totally melted. I'm not saying that Courtney killed Barbie, or even that she knows who did; I just find it interesting that she intentionally misled me about how long it had been since the two of them had spent time together."

"She might not want to get involved in the whole thing, but I suppose it wouldn't hurt to have a word with her anyway. I'll stop by to see if she tells me anything she didn't mention to you."

"I should get back to work. One of my new hires called in sick and I'm betting it's going to be a busy day. Call me if you have news."

"Okay, I will."

I headed back to my truck and considered what to do next. I could try to track down Phillip, but I had no idea where to find the delivery driver, and I knew that Courtney probably would be in the boutique she owned at this time of day. I called Jeremy to make sure there was nothing going on at the Zoo that he couldn't handle, then headed down the main thoroughfare on foot. I was halfway to my destination when I saw Veronica of Veronica's Bakery come running out of her shop with a blur of tan a second in front of her.

"Did you see that little thief?" she asked me. "I left the front door open to let in some fresh air and that mangy little dog came in and stole one of the baguettes right out of the display."

"He's been hanging around for the past couple of days," I acknowledged. "I'm sure he just smelled the wonderful aromas coming from your bakery and decided to grab some lunch."

"Are you going to go after him?"

I looked down the street. The dog and the bread were long gone. "I think he's gone for now, but I promise I'll look for him. It might be a good idea to keep your baked goods in a more secure location in the meantime. I ran his photo, and it doesn't seem anyone is looking for him, so my guess is that he's been on the street for a while."

Veronica looked down the street as if searching for the little tan dog. "I guess I don't mind that he took the bread. If he comes back around, I'll offer him a treat to see if I can catch him. If I do, I'll give you a call."

"Thanks. That would be very helpful."

After saying good-bye to Veronica, I continued on down the street. The boutique Courtney owned catered to women looking for designer clothing at discount prices. Most women went to the mall off the mountain to shop for that kind of thing, but Courtney's eye for style and her bubbly nature made her boutique a successful enterprise. The shop was designed to create a casual elegance that appealed to most women, even those, like myself, who were more interested in comfort than trendiness.

"Hey, Zoe. What brings you in today?" Courtney was a tall redhead with silky hair and long legs that seemed to go on forever. Her naturally thin frame provided the perfect canvas to show off the designer clothes she carried. Many women bought what she modeled hoping to end up looking like her, but the truth of the matter was, few women could pull off the sharp lines she tended to favor.

"Just browsing," I answered. I casually flipped through a rack of sleeveless sundresses in bright colors that would be fun to pair with the colorful sandals displayed in the shoe section of the upscale store.

"How did those outfits I helped you pick for your trip work out?" Courtney asked.

Courtney had selected several outfits for me to take on my trip to New York with Zak, which had been much appreciated because there's one thing I'm not, and that's a fashionista. "They were perfect. Thank you so much for taking the time to find the exact things I needed for the trip."

"I was happy to help. I guess now that you have a rich boyfriend, you'll need to update your wardrobe. Our new summer line has several items that would be perfect for you, if you want to try on a few things while you're here."

"I do need some new summer clothes," I began, "but I'm in a bit of a hurry today. I'm really here to ask about Barbie."

"I figured." The colorful bracelets on Courtney's arm clanked together as she lifted her hand to nervously tuck a strand of her long hair behind one of her diamond-studded ears. "Ellie was in yesterday. I'm really not sure what I can tell you. I have no idea who might have killed her or why."

"When was the last time you spoke to Barbie?" I asked.

Courtney hesitated. Ellie probably hadn't asked the question in quite as direct a fashion. Or if she had, perhaps Courtney was less comfortable lying to me. I was, after all, going to be one of her best customers if Zak continued to include me on his business trips.

"A while back," she answered vaguely. "Why?"

"Serenity mentioned that Barbie began acting odd back in March. They initially stayed in contact after Barbie left, but Serenity felt she was lying to her about the activities she'd gotten involved in, so she cut off all ties to her. I noticed this photo of you and Barbie—" I walked over to stand before the photo behind the counter—"which has to have been taken in the past month and figured you'd seen her more recently than she had. Serenity told me Barbie seemed to be into something seedy," I liberally paraphrased. "I was hoping you could tell me what that might have been."

Courtney began to fidget. I could tell she was uncomfortable with the question, so I decided to wait silently while she worked out what she wanted to say. I began to sift through a rack of brightly colored tops as I waited. I definitely could use some new clothes for summer. Courtney looked like she'd just stepped out of the pages of *Vogue*, while I looked more like someone who'd recently posed for a spread for *Field & Stream*. I glanced at myself in the full-length mirror near the dressing room and realized I really did need to update my look.

"Barbie met a new guy," Courtney began. "I'm not sure how she became involved with him, but I got the impression he was into something illegal. She never would fill me in on the specifics, but I think she'd begun to regret her choice."

"Serenity made a similar statement. She said Barbie met some people who had a plan to make a lot of money, but she had the impression the method they had in mind wasn't entirely legal. She also said Barbie had met a man, but there was a weird vibe about the whole thing."

"Yeah, that tracks," Courtney agreed. "Barbie came to see me a few weeks ago. She wouldn't tell me what was going on specifically, but she said she was in trouble and needed a place to hang out for a few days. I told her she could stay at my place as long as she wanted. I didn't mention that to Ellie because I'm fairly certain whatever Barbie was into was illegal, immoral, or both. I didn't want to sully her name."

"You're a good friend to want to protect her, but whatever she was into probably got her killed," I pointed out.

"Yeah, I thought about that after Ellie left. Still, I'm not sure Barbie would want me talking to either of you. I guess you know you weren't her favorite people."

"I know, but I want to find her killer. If you can think of anything that might help me . . ."

"I really don't know much," Courtney insisted. "Barbie showed up at my condo on a Monday three weeks ago. As I said, she needed a place to hang out for a while. I let her stay with me, but she insisted she didn't want to talk about whatever was going on. She was gone when I got home from work on Thursday and I never saw her again."

"She didn't come to see you when she was in town this past week?"

"No. I didn't even know she was here until someone mentioned it on Friday. I called her cell, but she didn't answer. I had a date Friday night, so I figured I'd try to catch up with her on Saturday, but she was already dead by then."

"When she came to see you a few weeks ago, how did she seem?"

"Scared. Other than the brief walk on the beach where that photo was taken, she never left the condo."

"And did she say anything at all about what was going on?"

"She said she met a guy who seemed really awesome at first but was turning out to be bad news. She wanted to break it off, but the dude was the possessive sort, so she needed to figure out how to make the break. I figured she was staying with me while she worked things out, so I was surprised when she left so abruptly."

"Did she mention the guy's name?" I asked.

"No, she seemed careful not to."

"And did she tell you why she left?"

"No. When I got home on that Thursday, I found a note that said she'd decided to go home and work things out, and that it would be better for both of us if I forgot she was ever here. I sort of think she was warning me that admitting she'd been here could put me in some sort of danger. I tried to call her several times, but she never answered or called me back."

"Do you know where she's been living since she left here in February?"

"She didn't say. I know it seems odd that she was here for three days, yet I know nothing, but she didn't want to talk about her life. The conversations we did have revolved around movies we'd seen or things we'd done in the past."

I walked across the shop and sat down on one of the chairs Courtney had placed outside of the dressing rooms. She had a flair for style, but these chairs had been selected for trendiness rather than comfort. Especially if you had short legs, which I do. I stood back up and leaned against the wall.

"At first I thought Barbie might have died at the hands of a past lover or a jealous wife," I said. "But I'm starting to think her death had more to do with what she got into after she left Ashton Falls than anything that might have occurred before she left."

"Maybe, though Barbie made a lot of enemies," Courtney admitted. "She seemed to like stirring things up. She'd flirt with some random guy and then wait for the wife or girlfriend to go ballistic. I think the fact that she could get any guy to pant after her gave her a sort of twisted thrill. I don't think she slept around quite as much as people assumed, though. It was usually enough for her to make the guy want her. She never took any of the guys she dated seriously. In fact, I think she considered most of them to be some sort of joke. The easier the guys succumbed to her wiles, the less respect she had for them. I knew her for quite a while, and the only guy I ever saw her really fall for was . . ."

"Levi," I supplied.

"Yeah, and what did that get her?"

My natural inclination was to jump in and defend my friend, but I realized that doing so would most likely end the conversation, so I bit my tongue . . . well, not literally.

"What about Brock?" I asked, mentioning the man Barbie had lived with prior to hooking up with Levi. "Have you heard from him lately?"

"Brock moved to Bryton Lake after he and Barbie split. I don't think they stayed in touch, although she might have gone to him if she were in trouble. I have his number if you'd like to contact him, though I'd appreciate it if you didn't mention that I gave it to you."

"Did Brock and Barbie end things on good terms?"

"Surprisingly, they did. I know Brock has a new girlfriend now, and I think they're pretty serious. Barbie knew about the relationship but didn't seem to care. I think their affair had run its course by the time they ended things."

"Okay, well, thank you for your time. And I really do need some clothes. You know my size and taste; why don't you pick out some things and I'll come by to try them on later in the week? Be sure to include a few of those tops I was looking at. Maybe lime green and lemon yellow. The mauve is nice as well, but no pink."

"Okay, I'll do that. And Zoe . . ."

"Yeah?"

"Be careful. Whoever killed Barbie is bad news. I wouldn't want to see you get hurt."

Chapter 10

After I left Courtney's, I returned to the Zoo. I'd left Charlie with Zak today and missed him desperately. I almost went by the house to pick him up but decided that a day apart wouldn't kill either of us. Still, I reasoned, it wouldn't hurt to call Zak to check up on things. Besides, Zak had promised to have a chat with Scooter's dad, and I'd been on pins and needles all morning, wondering how the conversation had turned out. I dialed Zak's cell number as soon as I arrived at the Zoo and said hi to Jeremy.

"How's my little guy?" I began.

"Little guy? I thought I was your *big* guy."

"Not you; Charlie," I clarified.

"Ah, I should have known you called to check up on your dog rather than your boyfriend."

"He's been in my life a lot longer," I teased.

"He's fine. The dogs and I went for a hike this morning, and now Lambda and Charlie are napping on the deck. How was your meeting?"

"Boring, but it looks like we have everything handled for the weekend. Did you have a chance to talk to Scooter's dad?"

"I did," Zak confirmed.

"And?" I began pacing nervously. If Zak couldn't work something out with Mr. Sherwood, there was a good chance poor Cody might be facing a death sentence.

"He agreed not to pursue a lawsuit or a complaint with the county."

I let out the breath I'd been holding for two days. "Did anyone ever tell you that you're an amazing man?"

"Actually, no."

"Well, you are. Thank you so much. Cody thanks you as well."

"Here's the thing . . ." Zak sounded hesitant.

"Thing?" I was afraid to ask.

"There was a price."

"He asked you for money? I figured he would. Whatever you had to pay the man was worth it. Cody doesn't deserve to die for protecting Sally."

"I agree. Cody doesn't deserve to die. That's why I agreed to the price. The thing is, Scooter's dad didn't ask for money."

"He didn't?" My heart started to pound. "What did he want?"

"A babysitter."

My heart sank into my shoes. "Babysitter?" I croaked.

"Scooter's dad has to go out of town for a few days, and he insisted that the only way he'd drop the whole thing is if I agreed to watch his kid."

"You didn't."

"You wanted to save the dog," Zak reminded me. "In fact, I seem to remember you asking me very nicely to do whatever it took."

"I was thinking of giving him money." I was starting to hyperventilate. "I wanted you to give him money."

"He didn't want money."

I reached for the chair behind me. I was pretty sure I was going to pass out. "Is he there now? At your house?" I clarified.

"He is."

"Oh, God," I groaned. "I hope your homeowner's insurance is paid up."

"It is," Zak assured me.

"What are we going to do with a kid? What are we going to do with *that* kid?" I emphasized.

"He's been here for over an hour. He went for a swim, and now he's playing video games. I think you're worrying for nothing."

I heard a crash in the background.

"I gotta go," Zak informed me. "Bring Cody when you come over."

"Cody?" I asked, but Zak had already hung up.

"What about Cody?" Jeremy poked his head into my office.

"Zak wants me to bring him to his house."

"I'm not sure you should do that. He's under unofficial quarantine."

"Scooter's dad is dropping the complaint," I informed Jeremy.

"That's great. What did Zak say to convince him?"

"He told Scooter's dad he'd babysit him."

"Babysit?" Jeremy said, the horror of the thought evident in his tone.

"Apparently, Scooter's dad had to go out of town for a few days."

"Poor Zak. Does he know what he's getting himself into?"

I remembered the crash. "If he didn't before, I'm pretty sure he does now."

"So if Scooter is at his house, why does he want you to bring Cody over?"

"I guess he's going to try to work out some sort of peace treaty between the two. I should call the Browns to let them know what's going on."

"I'm sure they'll be relieved that you figured out a way to get Cody off the hook, but be careful if you do decide to get Cody and Scooter together. Somehow I don't see Cody warming up to Scooter any time soon, and another bite could be bad news all around."

"Yeah, I'll take precautions. How did things go this morning?"

"Good. We arranged for an adoption for the last of the Birdwell kittens, and I've had four calls inquiring about the Lowery puppies. On the flip side, I've had two calls from families wanting to drop off kittens. I told them that we'd be happy to take them and offered them a coupon for a free spay. Both families are going to take me up on the offer. I have a call in to Scott to make arrangements for the mother cats."

"Excellent. How is Goliath doing this morning?"

"Better. His appetite is returning and he's starting to complain about his accommodations."

I smiled. "Excellent. We'll need to warn the others not to enter the cage without one of us, now that he's up and about. Scott seemed to think he'd recover quickly if we could get him up and eating. I'll need to talk to the forest service about a possible location to release him once the stitches come out."

"While you're at it, you might as well enter into a discussion about releasing the coyote pups. Now that the snow has melted and food sources are plentiful, I think they'll do fine on their own."

"Yeah, I will. Any other messages?"

"We had a call to pick up a stray bothering picnickers at Snowshoe Beach, but Tiff went ahead and took it. Other than that, it's been a quiet morning."

I picked up a stack of paperwork and headed down the hall toward the records room. Jeremy picked up his own pile and followed along behind me. "How's Morgan feeling this morning?" I knew Jeremy's month-old daughter had come down with a cold over the weekend.

"Better. Mrs. Broman has been a wonderful nanny. She knows exactly what to do in pretty much every situation. I don't know what I'd do without her. By the way, I'll need to leave early tomorrow, if that's okay. Mrs. Broman has a doctor's appointment."

"Sure, no problem. Did we get the ad in the weekend edition of the *Bryton Lake Courier* for the pet adoption?"

"Yeah, the proof is on your desk. They said the deadline for the ad is tomorrow, so they'd like you to get the proof back right away, if possible."

"I'll look at it as soon as I'm done here. Did you ask them about placement for the ad?"

"It's going to be featured on the weekend events page."

"Awesome. I'll be in my office if you need me."

I turned away and Jeremy returned to the front counter. The ad was colorful and appealing; Jeremy had done a good job with it. I was certain it would attract a lot of people to the adoption who otherwise might not have attended. The weekend events page was a color insert that was only printed on Fridays. I knew that the Events Committee had taken out an ad in the same insert for the Memorial Day festivities. The sales rep from the newspaper had suggested I pull up the special insert from a previous edition so I could consider the best placement for my ad. I logged into the site on my computer and entered the proper search command. I found the page that had run two weeks before. It featured a full-color ad showcasing an antiques auction that was to take place the following weekend, featuring a sampling of the items for sale, including an antique clock. Standing in the background behind the clock was none other than the late Barbie Bennington.

I remembered that Salinger had said he'd caught Barbie in the act of trying to steal an antique clock. I had to wonder if the clock in the photo and the clock she'd been attempting to steal were one and the same. Was it possible that Barbie, or someone associated with her, had sold the clock to the owner of One Man's Trash and then tried to steal it back? It made no sense that anyone would do such a thing, but the mere fact that an antique clock had been stolen the previous weekend and Barbie was then caught trying to steal it a few days later was too much of a coincidence to ignore. I printed the page, grabbed my purse, and headed out to Salinger's office.

"So you think this has something to do with Barbie's murder?" Levi asked later that afternoon, as I sat with him at his dining table and explained what I'd learned.

"I don't know. Maybe. I checked with Salinger, and he confirmed that the clock in the photo is the same one Barbie tried to steal. And I went to One Man's Trash and spoke to the owner, who confirmed that he had attended the sale and bought the clock, as well as several pieces of furniture, a few paintings, and a number of boxes of smaller household items. I offered to buy the clock, but he said he'd purchased it for his private collection and it wasn't for sale."

"So maybe Barbie tried to buy the clock, but he wouldn't sell it, so she tried to steal it," Levi theorized.

"Yeah, but why sell it in the first place?" I asked.

"Maybe she wasn't selling it. Maybe she was there to buy it," Levi suggested. "All we really know from the photo was that she was at the preview for the auction when the photo for the ad was taken. What if she was at the auction to buy the clock but lost the bidding to the antiques store owner?"

I frowned. "Does that clock seem like something Barbie would want?"

"No," Levi admitted.

"I suppose she could have been there to buy the clock on behalf of someone else. Several people I've talked to have suggested that Barbie was into something illegal. What if she's part of a group who uses antiques to make some sort of exchange?" I suggested.

"Exchange?"

"Yeah, like what if the clock has a secret compartment filled with drugs or diamonds or spy messages or something?"

"I think you've been watching too much television."

"Do you have a better explanation as to why Barbie a) attended the auction preview and b) broke into the antiques store and tried to steal the clock?"

Levi picked up the copy of the flyer I'd brought and looked at it again. It was clear that it was Barbie in the background. I'd called the auction company and confirmed that the preview had taken place over a three-day period from May 6 to 8. I knew the deadline to get an ad into the insert was the Wednesday prior to the Friday it was to be run, so the photo had to have been taken on Tuesday, the sixth. The auction had been held on Saturday, May 10, and according to Salinger, he'd found Barbie breaking into One Man's Trash on Wednesday, May 14. Barbie had called Levi on Thursday, May 15, and she'd drowned on the night of Friday, May 16. If she had indeed taken an ad out in the paper she'd sent to Levi, she'd most likely done so on Thursday, May 15.

"Wasn't there something about a sale or auction in the classified ads we were looking at?" I asked Levi.

He got up, walked across the room, which was cluttered with laundry and take-out containers, and picked up the paper. "Yeah," he replied. "There was an ad for an estate sale. The auction takes place this Thursday at 10 a.m."

"Maybe that's the clue," I suggested.

Levi frowned. "I don't think so. Remember, Barbie would have no way of knowing that we'd found out about her break-in or her attendance at the auction the previous weekend. Don't you think that if she was sending me a message, she'd send one I could figure out?"

"You have a point. If you were going to pick an ad, which one do you think she'd most likely send?"

Levi looked at the choices once again. There were two ads for vehicles for sale, two help-wanted ads, the ad for the estate sale, the ad for an antique cabinet for sale, and one for an apartment for rent. "The apartment," he finally decided. "She used to talk about us getting a bigger place, with a pool. The ad features an apartment that's exactly the type of place she used to talk about."

"Okay, so how did the game work? Was the message embedded in the text? Or could the message be to check out that specific location?"

Levi frowned. "In the movie, the message was a code embedded in the text." He looked at the ad more closely. "Nothing really pops, but maybe with a little more time . . ."

"Okay, you work on that. I really need to get home, and I still have to pick up Cody."

"Cody?"

"A dog with a record. I'll explain later. Call me if you figure anything out."

When I arrived at Zak's with Cody, Scooter was in the family room playing video games, which allowed me to introduce Cody to Zak and Lambda before the source of his angst was brought into the room. Cody was a sweet, well-adjusted dog who greeted both Zak and Lambda with enthusiasm. After we felt that Cody had adapted to his situation, I clipped a leash onto his collar, which I attached to a hook Zak had installed on the wall. I gave Cody a treat and a blanket to lay on and he settled right down. Zak went to fetch Scooter. At first, Cody just looked at Scooter as he trotted into the room. Zak instructed Scooter to have a seat at the table, which he did after only a small amount of negotiation. Charlie and Lambda were instructed to lay down on rugs of their own as the three of us settled down to eat. I slowly let out the breath I'd been holding as Scooter waited patiently for his food to be served.

"Can I have soda?" Scooter asked.

"I think milk would be better." Zak set a glass of milk in front of the child.

"I want soda." Scooter knocked over the glass with the swipe of his hand. The milk flowed everywhere, including into Scooter's lap. The kid jumped up and started screaming, which caused Cody to stand up and begin barking. Cody got the other dogs barking as well, and before you knew it, all hell had broken loose. Zak grabbed Scooter and headed toward the stairs, while I mopped up the spilled milk. By the time Zak returned, the dogs had calmed down, but dinner was ruined.

"Maybe I should take the dogs to the boathouse for the night," I suggested.

"That might be a good idea," Zak admitted. "Maybe you can drop Cody and Lambda off on your way into town tomorrow."

"Are you sure that trying to get Scooter and Cody together is a good idea? I mean, what if Cody bites Scooter again?"

"I'll be careful. Don't worry." He kissed my nose. "It will be fine."

I had serious doubts about that but agreed to Zak's plan. I kissed him and then headed toward my truck with all three dogs. If Scooter hadn't completely destroyed Zak's house by morning, I supposed we could try again.

Chapter 11

Wednesday, May 21

The next morning, I stopped by Zak's to drop off Lambda and Cody, as we'd discussed. I remembered that Jeremy was going to be in late due to Mrs. Broman's doctor's appointment, so I'd gotten an early start. Luckily, I decided to leave the dogs in the truck until I had a chance to check out the situation. When I opened the front door, I couldn't help but gasp. It looked like a tornado had blown through the place.

"What happened?" I asked Zak as he staggered into the room with a cup of coffee in his hand.

"Apparently, Scooter has some fairly strong opinions about such things as dishwashing, bathing, and bedtimes."

"I'm sorry." I put my hand over my mouth in an attempt to hide my smile. "I don't know why I'm laughing. This really isn't funny."

Zak looked around the room and smiled. "I guess it's a little funny."

We both broke out laughing. "How did that T-shirt end up hooked over the blade of the ceiling fan? The fan has to be at least twenty feet off the ground."

"Scooter has an excellent aim." Zak chuckled.

"As evidenced by the ketchup on your Mona Lisa print." I laughed harder. Luckily, the print was encased in glass and easily cleaned.

"Yes, well, you should see where his shoes ended up. The kid has a future in the NBA."

"Maybe I'd better just take Cody with me today," I said. "I can bring Lambda as well, if you'd like." I looked around the room, which was going to take most of the day to clean.

"No, I think things will be fine. Somewhere around two a.m., Scooter and I came to an understanding."

"You didn't hit him?"

"No," Zak assured me, "I didn't hit him. Let's just say I discovered his weak spot."

"Weak spot?" I was almost afraid to ask.

"The kid loves jets. I told him if he behaved while he was with me, I'd talk to his dad about taking him for a ride."

"You have a jet?" Zak had never mentioned having an airplane, but there was so much about his life outside of Ashton Falls that I was still discovering.

"No, but I have a friend who has one, and he owes me a couple of favors. I told Scooter that if he is cooperative and behaves himself for the remainder of his visit, I'd ask my friend to take us for a ride the next time he's in the area."

"I like jets," I offered. "Especially those heading toward exotic beaches." I began to imagine the possibility of running away to an exotic beach with Zak for a couple of days. I love my life and the people in it, but at times the distractions that come with having a full life can cut into the private time I want to spend with the man I love.

Zak pulled me into his arms and kissed me. "Maybe if you're a good girl . . ."

"Oh, I can be very good." I wrapped my arms around Zak's neck and then remembered that we had a nine-year-old in the house and took a step back. "Rain check?" I groaned.

"Definitely." Zak took a deep breath.

"Seriously, though," I refocused on the challenge at hand, "maybe I should just take Cody with me today. I'd hate to have another incident. You know what they say about three strikes."

"Don't worry. We'll be fine," Zak assured me again. "Is he in the truck?"

"Yeah."

"I'll walk out with you."

"Okay." I shrugged. "It's your funeral."

I arrived at the Zoo to find Tank, our nighttime staff, pacing back and forth in the hallway in front of the wild animal cages. "Something is wrong with Goliath," Tank informed me. "When I went in to feed him his breakfast, he was breathing but unresponsive."

"Did you call Scott?" I referred to our vet.

"He's on his way."

I left Charlie with Tank before heading to Goliath's cage. The staff was able to give Goliath food and water through a small window that allowed access to the cage without their having to actually enter the structure. Jeremy and I were the only two with the combination to open the door; we'd been trained to deal with wild animals, while the others had not. I grabbed a tranquilizer gun as a precaution and entered the enclosure. As Tank had indicated, Goliath was breathing but not conscious. I was kneeling down to check his heart rate when Scott came into the pen from the hallway.

"He's not responding to stimulation," I informed him.

"We'd better give him a sedative just to be safe," he cautioned. "Wouldn't want him waking up at an inopportune time."

Scott gave the mountain lion a shot, then knelt to check his vitals.

"Is he going to be okay?" I asked.

"It's too early to tell," Scott answered as he removed the cone from the animal's head, as well as the bandage he'd previously applied. "It looks like infection has set in. I'm going to give him some stronger antibiotics. We'll need to keep him sedated so we can monitor his progress. You'll need to give him injections every eight hours. I know you've given injections before, and I can show Tank and Gunner what to do, since they'll be here in the evenings."

"Is he dangerous?" I hated to think of Tank or Gunner, who really hadn't had a lot of training, having to deal with a cranky mountain lion.

"Not if you give him his injections on time. Don't miss one, though, because if he comes out of it, he could be extremely dangerous."

"Yeah, okay, we'll stay on top of it," I assured Scott.

"I'll be by after I close the clinic for the day to recheck his bandages," the vet informed me.

After Scott left, I did my rounds, checking on the rest of the animals. It was always tough when we lost one, especially a wild beauty like Goliath. Scott was an excellent vet and we were careful to follow his instructions, but every now and then Mother Nature took over, and despite our best efforts, we'd lose to nature's natural rhythm.

"How's he doing?" Tiffany asked when I joined her in the exercise area, where she was playing with several of the dogs.

"It's too soon to tell."

"He seemed much better yesterday. Is there something we could have done to prevent this from happening?"

Was there? I didn't know. Maybe if we'd monitored him more closely, or limited his mobility? Sometimes, in spite of doing everything right, some animals made it while others didn't. We'd had a dog the previous summer that had gotten into a tug-of-war with some rusted barbed wire. He was in pretty bad shape when he arrived, but he'd seemed to be doing better before taking a turn for the worse. He died in my arms two days after we'd taken him in.

"Zoe?" Tiffany asked when I didn't answer.

"Sorry. No, I don't think there was anything we could have done differently. We'll need to give him his injections and keep a close eye on him. Scott will be back later in the day to check on things."

"Poor Tank was a mess when he left. He feels like what happened to Goliath was his fault because he was supposed to be keeping an eye on him."

"I doubt there's anything Tank could have done. Sometimes these things just happen."

"I guess. Still, I hope we got to him in time. Scott had the same worried look in his eyes that he had when the golden retriever that was hit by the car on the highway was brought in."

"Scott's a good vet. If something can be done to save Goliath, I promise you it'll be done. All we can do is follow Scott's directions and keep an eye on him. I think I'll come back to take the night shift. If

Goliath wakes up, I'd prefer that I was the one who was here."

"Let me know if there's anything I can do," Tiffany offered. "Anything at all."

"Yeah, I'll let you know."

"Hey, Zoe," Jeremy interrupted. He'd come out into the yard, where Tiffany and I were talking, from the side door that can be accessed only by shelter staff. "I just got a call from the sheriff's office. They want someone to respond to the fire out on the highway to take possession of a couple of dogs."

"Fire?"

"That old junkyard on the way out of town. Guess someone torched it."

"One Man's Trash?" I wondered.

Jeremy shrugged. "I guess. I can go, if you want."

"No, that's okay, I'll go. I'll leave Charlie with you, though. I wouldn't want him getting underfoot."

As I pulled my truck onto the highway and began traveling north, I could see a plume of smoke in the distance. I called my dad, a volunteer firefighter who has shifted from fighting fires to manning the control center as he's gotten older. He confirmed that the antiques store had all but burned to the ground. According to Dad, the store had been closed and the owner was yet to be located. Luckily, the fire department had arrived in time to rescue the two guard dogs that were locked in the gated area surrounding the store. The fire had completely destroyed not only the main building but the out buildings that were also on the premises.

"Arson?" I asked the deputy in charge after taking possession of the two dogs and securing them in my truck.

"Too early to tell for certain, but based on the heat of the thing, I think it's likely."

I watched as the fire department continued to spray thousands of gallons of water on the structure, even though there wasn't really anything left to save.

"Anyone caught inside?" I hoped not. If someone had been trapped inside when the fire started, they were most likely dead now.

"As far as we can tell, the place was unoccupied at the time the fire ignited. Good thing we got here when we did or those dogs would be crispy critters."

I grimaced at the thought. "Is Salinger around?"

"He was here, but he headed back into town. We mostly just have clean up at this point."

"Excuse me, Deputy Collins, but one of my men found something just outside the perimeter of the property that we think you should see."

"What is it?" the deputy asked.

"Well . . ." The firefighter looked at me and hesitated.

"Spit it out. What's so important that you'd interrupt my conversation with this pretty lady?"

Oh, please. The guy was a total tool. Was everyone who was employed by the Ashton Lake branch of the Bryton Lake Sheriff's Department a moron?

"We found the owner of the building, sir. He's in the forest, just beyond the fence. He's been shot. He's alive, but barely. A couple of the guys are with him. We've called an ambulance."

"Well, why didn't you say so in the first place?" The deputy hurried off toward the location the volunteer fireman had indicated.

The firefighter shook his head and looked at me. "And I'm the one volunteering my time while he's getting paid."

"Did the man look like he'd been shot where the body was found?" I asked.

"No, ma'am. He'd definitely been moved."

Ma'am? Really?

"I need to get back," the man informed me. "You'd best stand back out of the way. What's left of the building is going to collapse any minute now."

"Okay, I'll be going." I paused. "I'm sorry I don't know your name. I'm Zoe Donovan."

"Hank's daughter?"

"That'd be me."

The man held out a hand blackened by soot. "Happy to meet you. I've heard a lot about you. My name is Trevor Seymore. I just moved to the area a month ago."

"Happy to meet you as well, Trevor."

After dropping the dogs off at the Zoo, I continued into town in the hope of having a conversation with Salinger. If the owner of One Man's Trash had bought the clock at the auction, and if Barbie had indeed broken in to steal the clock, then it made sense that the clock could in some way be related to her death. Of course, if the clock was destroyed in the fire, we had little chance of using it as a means of pulling this whole mystery together.

The fact that the owner of One Man's Trash was shot and then dumped in the woods seemed to indicate that someone had picked up where Barbie left off. My best guess was that the owner had interrupted whomever had broken in and been shot for his efforts. I'd called the hospital and was informed that the man was alive but not yet conscious. Perhaps if and when he woke up, he'd be able to fill in a few of the blanks. I half-expected Salinger to be out investigating the attempted murder of the shop owner, but when I arrived at the sheriff's office he was alone in his office. His secretary wasn't at her desk, so I knocked on his door and was waved in.

"I take it you heard about the fire?" Salinger asked as I sat down on one of the hard plastic chairs lining the wall.

"I was called in to pick up the owner's dogs. It looks like someone finished what Barbie started."

"Perhaps," Salinger acknowledged. "At this point, we don't have any information about the cause of the fire, nor do we have any suspects in the shooting of the store owner. I would appreciate it if you'd refrain from making a connection between Ms. Bennington's death and what happened this morning until we know more."

"You think there's a possibility they might not be related?"

"I think we don't know enough to make that leap. Unsubstantiated theories can only hurt the investigation if they're made public. At this point only you and I know that Ms. Bennington broke into the place before her death. I'd like to keep it that way."

"And Levi, Zak, and Ellie."

"What about Levi, Zak, and Ellie?"

"You said only you and I knew about Barbie's break-in. I wanted to clarify that Levi, Zak, and Ellie knew as well."

Salinger frowned. "I really wish you hadn't told them."

"I told you that I don't keep secrets from them. Don't worry, they won't say anything. They've been helping with the investigation."

"And have you found out anything?"

"Perhaps." I showed him the ad for the antiques auction and shared with him our theory that Barbie's death must in some way be tied into her presence at the auction, as well as her attempt to steal the clock. Salinger didn't seem thrilled by what I'd found out, but he did say that he'd look into it and let me know what, if anything, he discovered. He assured me of his intention to find out exactly who had bought the clock, as well as who'd offered the clock for sale in the first place.

I was moderately pacified by his assurances, so I returned to the Zoo to check on our sick mountain lion.

Chapter 12

Once I returned to the Zoo, I went through the motions of my day. I cleaned pens and fed animals. I processed adoption applications and finalized our ad for the adoption clinic the following weekend. Goliath seemed to be resting comfortably, although his respiration was shallow and irregular at times. Scott came back and declared him stable. After quite a bit of discussion, we decided that Tiffany would stay with Goliath while I went to check on things at Zak's, and then I would come back to stay overnight to keep an eye on our patient. I had medical training that Tank and Gunner didn't, and given the nature of the situation, I didn't feel it was right to ask one of the employees to administer the two a.m. shot.

I'm not sure what I expected when I let myself in Zak's front door. Possibly another Armageddon. What I was greeted with instead was a clean and organized home and absolute silence. "Zak," I called as I made my way through the house. Somehow, Zak had even managed to get the T-shirt off the fan. The sound of laughter from the back of the house led me in that direction. I walked out onto the back deck to find Zak and Scooter paddling around in Zak's two-man kayak. Scooter was laughing at something Zak was telling him, and the two of them looked like they were having a fantastic time. Zak waved at me when he saw me standing on the deck and started paddling toward shore.

"Did you see me?" Scooter asked as he hopped out of the boat before Zak had even pulled it all the way onto the sand.

"I did. It looked like you were having fun," I answered as Cody and Lambda trotted over to greet the paddlers. I held my breath as Cody approached Scooter and the boy leaned in for a hug.

"Zak showed me how to paddle the kayak. He's gonna teach me to use the stand-up paddle board tomorrow."

"Do you know how to swim?" Stand-up paddle boarding can be difficult to learn, and more often than not, a novice will spend a good amount of time in the water.

"Yeah, my mom taught me before she died."

"Can you stay for dinner?" Zak gave me a quick peck on the cheek.

"We's having pizza," Scooter informed me.

"Pizza sounds good. How about I call and order it while the two of you get changed?" I volunteered.

"Just cheese," Scooter declared. "I don't want no olives or other stuff."

"Just cheese it is." I looked at Zak. "Any preference on a second selection?"

"Whatever you want is fine. Don't forget to wash your feet in the outdoor shower," Zak reminded Scooter as he trotted toward the house with the dogs on his heels.

"What did you do to that kid?" I asked as Scooter washed and dried his feet before heading inside.

"We just had a man-to-man talk." Zak pulled the kayak up toward the house. "He's had a tough time of it. First his mom dies unexpectedly, and then his dad goes off the deep end and basically stops parenting. I think his misbehavior is really just an attempt to get the attention he's been lacking."

"He seems like a different kid than the one I had dinner with yesterday," I admitted. "And he seems to be getting along with Cody."

"Cody is a good dog. Once Scooter settled down, Cody settled down. I talked to Sally's dad. He's going to bring Sally by tomorrow after school. We thought it would be good to see how Cody responds to Scooter with Sally in the picture. I told him that he could take Cody home with him after the visit. I hope that's okay. It seems Sally has been beside herself since the biting incident."

"Yeah, that should be fine."

"We decided that we'd arrange for Cody and Sally to meet up with Scooter and me on the street somewhere on Friday to see how Cody responds in that situation. Hopefully, all will go well and we'll see the last of Cody's biting spree."

"You've really worked wonders with that kid." I kissed Zak on the lips. He was going to make some kid a great dad one day.

"Where's Charlie?" Zak had noticed that he wasn't by my side.

"I left him in the truck until I had a chance to check out the situation. I'll go and get him before I call for the pizza."

"And I'll go and change while you do that."

I went back to the truck to get Charlie, who had been waiting patiently, before returning to the house and ordering the pizza. I decided to make a salad to go with the pizza and began digging through Zak's refrigerator to find the fixings. Zak did a much better job of keeping his kitchen stocked with fresh food than I did. It isn't that I don't appreciate fresh fruits and vegetables, it's more that I rarely take the time to go to the grocery store until I'm out of pretty much everything.

I could hear Zak and Scooter talking in the living room as I worked. It sounded like they were trying to decide on a video game to play while they were waiting for the pizza. I rummaged through the refrigerator until I found the bottle of Pinot we'd opened a few days earlier. If I was going to be ignored, I supposed I could have a glass of excellent wine while I waited.

"Pizza ordered?" Zak walked into the kitchen.

"It should be here in about an hour. I'm making a salad to go with it."

"I have a new salad dressing I've been wanting to try," Zak informed me. "The man at the farmers market assured me it's made fresh weekly."

"You went to the farmers market?"

"Yeah. I try to go every week during the season. Didn't you notice all the fresh produce?"

"I did, but I thought it was from the market."

Zak sliced the tomato I'd placed on the cutting board. He sliced off a chunk and fed it to me. "That's delicious," I had to admit.

"Farm fresh is the best. I'll pick you up some stuff to keep on hand at the boathouse when I go next week. They have those olives you love, and I know that corn on the cob is your favorite. They have locally brewed beer as well."

"Maybe I can take some time off and go with you," I suggested.

"Sounds like a date."

"Did you hear about the fire at One Man's Trash?"

"Yeah, I picked it up on the scanner."

"You have a police scanner?"

"It's a hobby."

I frowned. How could I have practically lived in this house for over a month and not known that? I really did need to learn to pay better attention. Levi and Ellie both insisted that Zak was more invested in our relationship than I was. I liked to deny that fact, but the truth of the matter was that he knew everything about me and I was constantly amazed to find out new things about him.

"Did you hear anything interesting?" I wondered.

"Just that they're pretty sure the fire was set intentionally, and that the man who was shot is on life support. I heard them mention that the dog lady was on her way, so I figured you might know more than me."

"I was called in to pick up the owner's dogs, but I don't know much. My guess is that the fire and the attempted murder of the shop owner is tied into Barbie's death in some way. If I had to guess, someone picked up where Barbie left off and broke in to steal the clock. The store owner caught him and was shot for his effort. I imagine the fire was set to destroy any evidence that might have been left behind in the store."

"Sounds like a good theory. Have you spoken to Salinger?" Zak asked.

"Yeah. He wants me to stay quiet about my ideas until he can investigate. Part of me feels like I should drop everything and dig into it while the trail is hot, but I have a sick mountain lion to worry about, so my plan is to leave Salinger to his investigation for the time being. Who knows, maybe he'll turn something up. If not, I guess there's always tomorrow."

"Speaking of tomorrow, I thought I'd take Scooter to the mall in Bryton Lake to do some shopping. He needs some new clothes. We thought we'd make a day of it, maybe take in a movie or check out that new arcade. I know you have book club tomorrow night, so I figured you'd be otherwise occupied anyway."

"Sounds like fun, although I'm not sure I'll have the energy to attend book club. I'm staying over at the Zoo tonight, so I'll see how it goes."

Chapter 13

Thursday, May 23

After I returned to the Zoo, I tried to sleep but ended up pacing until it was time to give Goliath his shot. I grabbed the tranquilizer gun as a precaution, in case he should wake from his deep sleep, and let myself into the cage. I administered the sedative as well as the antibiotic and rechecked his vitals, as Scott had shown me how to do. He seemed to be resting more comfortably than he had been earlier in the day. His heartbeat was strong and his respiration steady. I checked his bandage, which appeared to be clear of seepage from the wound Scott had needed to reopen earlier in the day.

I returned to the converted storage room we'd been using for Tank and Gunner's overnight shifts and found Charlie sleeping on the cot. I hadn't stopped to consider how uncomfortable the thing was until I was faced with sleeping on it and vowed to look into the purchase of a proper bed the next day. I'd brought a couple of books but found my attention wandering. It had been a long and emotional day. I knew I needed to sleep, but the harder I tried to drift into slumber, the more dreamland eluded me. Finally, I got up and switched on my computer. If I couldn't sleep, I might as well see if I could find out anything new.

I began by pulling up the ad I'd come across on Tuesday. Barbie was definitely standing in the background, but there were several other people in the ad as well. I tried to decide whether I recognized anyone else in the photo. There was a woman with short blond hair wearing a deep blue suit in the foreground. I didn't think I knew her, though there was something about her that seemed familiar. She was holding a plate that looked to be from a set of antique china, but rather than looking at the china in her hand, she appeared to be looking at something or someone in front of her, out of camera range.

Barbie stood behind her, off to the right. She was looking into the distance as well. If I had to guess, both women were looking at the person who took the photo, but it could just as well have been another person or even an object that held their attention. Just to the left of Barbie was a man in a dark-colored suit. The man was far enough away so that he was out of focus, so I couldn't make out any distinguishing features, other than the fact that he was tall and had dark hair. The only other person in the photo was a man who seemed to be familiar with auctions in general. He was perfectly groomed and well-dressed but had an unmistakable look of boredom on his face.

I knew the preview had lasted three days, with two hours set aside on each of those days for potential buyers to check out the items to be auctioned, so chances were many people had attended the event. I was interested to see what, if anything, Salinger would find out that might help us narrow things down a bit.

After studying the photo for so long that my eyes began to water, I decided to try to search for evidence of Barbie's life over the past three months. I don't know what I hoped to find, since neither Zak nor

Salinger had been able to uncover anything, but I was bored and antsy, and it gave me something to do. After two hours of searching, I was on the verge of giving up when I came across a photo of an auction in a town four hours to our north. Standing in the background was Barbie with the man Ellie and I had come to think of as lifeguard guy. I scrolled back to the original photo and realized that the man who was out of focus in it shared features similar enough to lifeguard guy that it was arguable that it was the same man in both photos. I didn't know what, if anything, that might mean, but I figured it might be worth our while to find out who exactly lifeguard guy was, and why he happened to be with Barbie not only at the auction but on the day she died.

At some point I drifted off to sleep and ended up with my head on the keyboard, which is where Jeremy found me. He sent me home to get some sleep, and by the time I woke up it was well into the afternoon. There were three messages from Levi, asking me to meet him at Ellie's Beach Hut after I got off work, which gave me time to grab a quick shower before heading out.

"Levi called and said he had a stop to make, so he'll be a little late," Ellie informed me shortly after I arrived. "Have you eaten?"

"No, and I'm starving. Mountain lion sitting is stressful work."

"How is Goliath?"

"Better. We had an uneventful night, and Jeremy called to say that Scott stopped in shortly after I left. He's doing much better, so they're going to cut back on the sedative and try to get some food into him."

"I'm so happy to hear that," Ellie said, then glanced across the deck. "It looks like the couple at table five are getting up. Go on out and grab it, and I'll bring you a sandwich."

"With potato salad," I requested.

I tossed the empty take-out containers the people had left into the trash before sitting down at the table overlooking the beach. It was another beautiful day in paradise. The sun shone brightly on the clear aqua-blue water that was dotted with sailboats out for an afternoon cruise. During the summer, the beach on this part of the lake is so crowded you can hardly see the sand, but at this time of year, only a few families venture out on a Thursday afternoon.

Ellie set a sandwich and potato salad in front of me, along with my favorite microbrew. "Can you believe that the Memorial Day weekend events start tomorrow?"

"I had a momentary panic attack earlier in the day, but I went over everything in my mind and I think we're ready. I've confirmed the vendors for the kiddie carnival. Willa volunteered to check everyone in tomorrow morning. I figured they could start setting up in the park as early as ten since the carnival doesn't start until three. The food vendors are likewise confirmed, and Jeremy promised he had a handle on the pet adoption before I agreed to go home this morning."

"It's supposed to be a really nice weekend. I'm betting we can expect a good turnout," Ellie added. "I posted flyers all over town and took out ads in all of the newspapers within a hundred miles. I'm really excited to bring Hannah to the kiddie carnival. Kelly is going to cover the Beach Hut for the weekend, so we can spend some quality mother-daughter time."

"Don't you think Hannah is a little young to throw darts at balloons or toss a ring over a bowling pin?" I watched as a group of kids chased a dog with a towel in his mouth down the beach.

"Maybe, but she can hold a pole at the fishing booth and pick a duckie out of the duck pond. She's going to love it. Kids are so much fun."

"If you say so." It's not that I don't like kids; it's just that I find kids—except for Harper, of course—somewhat terrifying.

"How is your own little delinquent doing?" Ellie said, referring to Scooter.

"Actually, when I went by Zak's for dinner last night, the two of them were having a blast. It looked like they'd negotiated some sort of truce and then spent the day doing the male-bonding thing. Zak took Scooter shopping today, and they planned to hang out tonight. I think Zak is really enjoying his babysitting duty, and Cody and Scooter are now friends, so that's one catastrophe averted. Zak called earlier and said that Cody's home with his family and everyone involved is happy."

"That's wonderful. Zak's going to make some lucky kid a great dad," Ellie commented.

"Yeah," I agreed. "He really is."

"Maybe you and Zak can bring Scooter to the weekend events."

"Zak might want to, but I'm going to be pretty busy. Not only do I have to oversee the kiddie carnival, but I have the pet adoption clinic and the water show to worry about."

"Relax. You just finished telling me the kiddie carnival was all but handled and Jeremy was on top of the pet adoption. I sort of forgot about the water show, though. Are you and Levi going to be ready?" Ellie asked.

"We'll do fine. We haven't really had time to practice, but we've been skiing and boarding together since we were kids. We have a rhythm. I just hope Levi isn't too distracted by this murder investigation to focus on what he's doing. I'd hate to get our lines tangled in midair."

"He did sound sort of off when I spoke to him earlier," Ellie said. "I'm sure he isn't getting a lot of sleep. He had this almost manic tone to his voice."

"Yeah, that's what I was afraid of."

"So what did you think of that buffalo chicken?" Ellie asked as I finished off the sandwich she'd brought me.

"It was good. It seemed like it needed something, though."

"That's what I was thinking too."

"Maybe try blue cheese crumbles in a ranch dressing rather than using blue cheese dressing. And maybe trade pepper jack cheese for the regular jack. And bacon," I added. "You can never go wrong with bacon."

"If you had your way, I'd put bacon on everything," Ellie teased.

"Hey, guys." Levi sat down next to me. He looked like hell. His eyes were bloodshot, and it looked like he hadn't combed his hair in days. Levi is usually meticulous about his hair.

"Are you okay?" I asked.

"Yeah. Fine. Just had a late night, but I think I might be onto something."

"How about something to eat before we get into this," Ellie suggested.

"Eat?" Levi looked confused.

"Nourishment," Ellie teased. "I can grill you a burger."

Levi looked toward the industrial-size BBQ Ellie had installed on the outdoor deck. "Yeah, okay. I guess I could use a burger."

Ellie got up to toss a patty on the grill.

"Where's Zak?" Levi asked me.

"He's hanging out with Scooter."

"Scooter?"

I explained about the babysitting job Zak had agreed to in an attempt to save Cody.

"Way to sacrifice yourself," Levi commented.

"Things started off a little rough, but I think Zak and Scooter are bonding. Scooter has had a tough time since his mom died. I think maybe he just needed a patient and stable adult in his life—who happened to have access to a jet."

"A jet?"

I explained about the deal the two had struck on that first night.

"I'm glad Zak saved Cody and, apparently, saved Scooter too in the process, but I was hoping to tap into his superior intelligence to help us solve the puzzle I think I uncovered."

"Hey, I have superior intelligence. Hit me."

"Okay." Levi shrugged and unfolded the paper Barbie had sent him. It was so worn and tattered, it appeared he must have read it a few thousand times. "I started to think about the conversations Barbie and

I had in the past. It didn't make sense that she would send me a message I couldn't figure out, so the clue in the paper had to be something that would have meaning to me but not to others."

"Makes sense."

"I went back over the ads that were placed on Thursday. Given what we'd found out about Barbie's participation in the auction at which the clock she tried to steal was sold, the ad for the estate sale or perhaps the antique cabinet for sale seemed the best fit. The thing is that Barbie had no way of knowing we'd find out about the clock and the auction. Logic would dictate that her clue would be placed in an ad I would associate with her. From the first my gut told me that the ad for the apartment was my best bet. Barbie was really pushing for us to move in together prior to the spilt, and there were a few occasions when we actually talked about the type of place we'd look for. The ad seemed to meet our wish list, up to and including the nook in the kitchen. I spent an ungodly number of hours trying to find a code within the text since that was the way it worked in the movie. After hours and hours of coming up blank, I noticed that the ad didn't provide a phone number but rather a post office box where inquiries were to be sent. I realized that was strange in and of itself; usually an ad for an apartment for rent would provide an address, or at least a phone number. I went to the post office and located the box. It was one of the temp boxes with combination locks the person who pays for the box can input. After about twenty tries, I figured out that Barbie had used my birthday. I opened the box and found this inside."

Levi handed me the flyer I'd found online that showed her at the auction preview, with the clock in the foreground. "So she wanted you to know about the auction," I realized. "But why?"

"There's a number written on the back of the flyer. It took me a while to figure this out, but each item in the auction is assigned a lot number. We need to find out what item this number was associated with for this particular auction."

"And then what?" I asked. "Let's say the item leads to the clock. We already know the antiques store has been burned to the ground, so any clue we might gain is long gone."

"Yeah." Levi sighed. "But it's the only lead we have. And maybe the number doesn't lead to the clock. Maybe it leads to something else. Or, more importantly, *someone* else. I hoped Zak would be here so he could use his magic computer to find out what item was associated with this number."

"Have you tried calling the auction house?" I asked.

"No, but I doubt they'd give me any information."

"Perhaps, but it never hurts to try."

Ellie returned with Levi's burger. I spent the next twenty minutes trying to get through to the newspaper in the hope of gaining the name and phone number for the auction house that had placed the ad. After I'd spoken to the third person, I came away with the information I needed. Ellie gave Levi a slice of the chocolate sundae pie she'd made while I called the auction house. Luckily, someone answered. I tried to channel Bitzy Bellingham as I slipped into my upper-class accent, which was basically my own tinged with a blend of boredom and indifference.

"Finally," I drawled, even though the woman who answered the phone did so on the third ring. "I hope you can help me. I sent my idiot buyer's agent to your little auction a few weeks ago to procure a specific item and the dolt came home with the wrong thing."

"I'm sorry to hear that," the woman answered politely.

"I'm trying to track the item down and hoped you'd be a dear and provide me with the contact information for the person who bought it."

"I'm really not at liberty to give out that information."

"I'm sure. However, in this instance, I'm certain you can make an exception. You see, my elderly mum had her eye on it, and Mum has a way of getting what Mum wants. I'd be willing to pay the winning bidder three times the price he obtained it for, plus a nice finder's fee for yourself, of course."

The woman hesitated. I could picture her greedy self punching it out with her moral self.

"The item number was C74-283."

"Hang on." The woman put me on hold. I hoped she was looking it up and not calling security.

Several minutes later, she came back on the line. "The item in question was purchased by a retailer rather than a private buyer," she informed me. "I tried to contact him—retailers often welcome a deal such as the one you're offering—but he didn't answer. The painting you're looking for was purchased by an antiques shop near Ashton Falls. The name of the shop is One Man's Trash. I have the address, if you'd like.

A painting? "I'd appreciate it."

The woman gave me the phone number and address, which I realized was useless, now that the place had burned to the ground.

"The number on the flyer matched the item number for a painting," I informed Levi.

"I thought Barbie tried to steal a clock."

"Maybe the clock was a diversion," Ellie suggested.

"That makes no sense," Levi argued.

"Maybe it does," I said. "What if Barbie was in the store to steal the painting? She hears Salinger come in the front and grabs the first thing she can find, pretending to be stealing it. If she was after the painting, her ploy would mislead whomever caught her. Maybe she stayed in town, figuring she'd try again later, but was killed before she could finish her mission."

"Or maybe she did get back in and was able to retrieve whatever it was she was after but was killed anyway," Levi added.

"I don't think so. Let's look at the timeline. Barbie was photographed at the auction preview on Tuesday, May 6th. We know this because the preview times were from three to five on May 6th, 7th, and 8th, but the deadline for placing the ad in the paper was noon on the seventh. The auction was held on Saturday, May 10th. I guess we can assume that Barbie was supposed to buy the painting. For some reason we don't yet know, she failed to make the purchase. The new owner took the painting back to his shop. Barbie breaks in on Wednesday, May 14th, to steal the painting. Salinger sees the light and comes in through the front. Barbie picks up the clock and pretends to be stealing it."

"And Salinger escorts her out before she can get what she came for," Ellie added.

"She called me on the morning of the 15th," Levi supplied. "Maybe after her evening with Salinger, she decided she'd had enough and wanted out of whatever it was she was into. She hoped I'd help her, but I blew her off and she ended up dead. God, I suck."

I put my hand over Levi's and gave it a squeeze. "She had to have placed the ad shortly after she spoke to you to get it in the weekend edition," I continued. "I guess we can suppose she put the flyer in the post office box that morning as well."

"We saw her at the beach on Friday," Ellie contributed. "She was there most of the day, so we can assume she hadn't as of yet completed the task she was in town for. It seems like if she'd accomplished her mission, she would have taken off rather than continued to hang around. What I don't get is, if she was in trouble, why didn't she go to someone else for help after Levi refused to meet with her? Courtney had helped her once before, and Serenity probably would have helped her out as well."

"Maybe someone showed up after her failed attempt on Wednesday to keep an eye on things," I suggested.

"Lifeguard guy," Ellie speculated. "He didn't leave her side all day, but they didn't appear to be on intimate or even friendly terms."

"How do you know that?" Levi asked.

Ellie blushed. I was certain she wouldn't want to admit she'd spent the day spying on Barbie.

"Ellie was working the pier that day," I said, diving in for the rescue. "I'm sure she can't help but notice what's going on down on the beach."

"Yeah, okay, so this man you both refer to as lifeguard guy was with her. Maybe he killed her."

"Maybe he did," I agreed.

"One Man's Trash burned down this past Wednesday. I suppose that after Barbie was killed, someone else broke in to finish the job, then torched the place," Ellie added.

"Okay. Say all of this is true; how can this help us prove who killed Barbie?" Levi asked.

"And there are a lot of other unanswered questions," I pointed out.

"Like what?" Ellie asked.

"If lifeguard guy did kill Barbie, why kill her on the same beach where thousands of people had seen them together the entire day? Why not do the deed at another time or place where you wouldn't be linked with the victim?"

"And it's always bothered me that Barbie was found in the water near the pier in that expensive dress and three-inch heels," Levi added. "Someone must have lured her there. There is no way she'd intentionally dress that way to party at the lake. For one thing, it was cold. Too cold for that dress."

"True. Barbie must have been elsewhere that evening. Maybe we can ask around and find out where," I suggested.

"Yeah, and maybe we can find out who she was with," Levi added.

"So what now?" Ellie asked. "Do we take this to Salinger?"

"Maybe we should," I said.

"Do we really trust him?" Levi asked. "I mean, in a way, he's involved in this whole thing. What if he killed Barbie to protect his secret?"

"I'm not a huge fan of the guy, but I doubt he'd actually kill anyone."

"Zoe is right," Ellie added. "I don't think Salinger would go that far."

"Personally, I don't think I can sit in the same room with the man after what he did to Barbie," Levi declared.

"I'll stop by Salinger's office on my way to book club," I offered, "which I'm going to be late to if I don't get going."

"Yeah, I need to get going too," Ellie added. "Rob and I have a date. We're going to talk about the wedding. I think I've pretty much narrowed it down to a few weeks in either July or August. It would be nice to make the move to his house while the weather is nice and besides, my lease is up on September 1st. It doesn't make sense to either renew it or look for another place."

"You could just move in together and worry about the wedding at another time," I pointed out.

"Yeah, we could do that, but I think I'm ready to have this over with."

I frowned. That didn't sound like a statement a woman who couldn't wait to spend her life with the man of her dreams would make.

"Will you be okay?" I asked Levi. "I can call Pappy and tell him I can't make it to book club if you want to hang out."

"No, that's okay. What I really need is some sleep. I'll catch up with you tomorrow."

Chapter 14

My Thursday night book club actually started off as an offering through the senior center. Over the course of the past year, it has evolved into a much smaller group that meets in the home of one of our members. This week it was Hazel Hampton's turn to host the event. Hazel is single and serves our community as both librarian and as a member of the Events Committee I belong to. There has been a rumor circulating around town that Hazel and Pappy, my grandpa, have been "keeping company" with each other for the past several months. Neither Hazel nor Pappy has come out and stated as much, but I have to admit that they do seem to be spending quite a bit of time together as of late.

Hazel lives in a small house just a few blocks from Main Street. Like many of the homes in that neighborhood, Hazel's yard is bordered by a freshly painted white picket fence. The exterior of the house is painted a pale yellow with white trim that perfectly matches the white of the wooden shutters that frame each window.

As I pulled up in front of the charming cottage, I noticed that Hazel's yellow vine rose was in full bloom. It always amazed me that her roses bloomed months before the others in town, but Hazel explained that the variety she chose was an early bloomer she keeps warm in a homemade greenhouse structure of sorts during the cold winter months. Whatever she does, the affect is striking. Thousands of tiny yellow flowers that reminded me of crepe paper covered the healthy vines that grew on trellises along the front walkway. Hazel has a yard service that comes by twice every week to ensure that the lawn is perfectly groomed and the flowerbeds free of weeds.

I called Charlie to my side as we made our way up the rose-covered walkway. It really was magical to walk under the dome of yellow roses, which seemed to attract a number of hummingbirds that fluttered around from one flower to another. I admired the flowers displayed in brightly painted pots as I waited on the porch for Hazel to answer the bell. Some of the members of the book club simply leave a note on the door inviting people to come on in, but Hazel is a tad more formal than that.

"Zoe, I'm so glad you could come," Hazel, wearing a yellow sundress, greeted me. I couldn't help but notice that her dress matched her house exactly. Leave it to Hazel to coordinate.

"I hope it's okay that I brought Charlie." I was certain it would be, but with Hazel it's never a waste of time to be polite.

"Certainly." Hazel smiled at Charlie. I don't know a lot about Hazel's past, but I'd be willing to bet that she was raised in a prim and proper upper-class household. I don't know for certain whether she has ever been married. She's been single since moving to Ashton Falls and appears to be childless, given the fact that neither children nor grandchildren are ever mentioned. "We are in the family room. Go on back and make yourself comfortable."

I entered the room to find that Phyllis King, Nick Benson, Pappy, and our newest member, Ethan Carlton, had already arrived. By the time we'd all greeted each other, Hazel returned with Lilly Evans on her heels. Lilly had been one of our original members who stopped attending for a while but then rejoined the group after a couple of members she didn't get along with moved on. I like Lilly. I really do. But the woman can be somewhat pushy and opinionated. If she likes you, she's sweet as pie. If she doesn't . . . well, let's just stay that I work hard to remain on her good side.

"Please help yourself to refreshments before we begin," Hazel announced. It appeared that she had gone to a lot of trouble to prepare home-baked pastries to serve with her freshly brewed coffee. "The éclairs are my specialty, so be sure to try one."

I had to admit the pastries were really good. As I helped myself to my third éclair, I realized I'd have to ask Hazel for the recipe; I was pretty sure I was addicted by that point.

"How's the investigation going?" Nick Benson walked up beside me and began filling his plate.

Nick is a good foot and a half taller than I am, so I needed to look up before answering. "How do you know I'm investigating?"

"Everyone knows your investigating," Nick responded.

I considered the man with his full head of thick brown hair that had just begun to turn gray in spite of the fact that he was well into his sixties. "I guess it's going okay. I'm not sure that we're any closer to proving who killed Barbie than we were when we started, but I feel like we're narrowing down our list of suspects. I had a conversation with Salinger, and he's going to look into a few things."

"So you're working together on this one?"

"I guess we are. It's kind of an odd case."

"Odd how?" Nick wondered.

I glanced around the room. If I explained the complexities to Nick, I knew I'd end up involving everyone else as well. On one hand, Salinger probably wouldn't want me talking about a case that he'd yet to solve, but on the other, the room was filled with intelligent people who might very well offer input on the situation that neither Salinger nor I had yet to consider. In addition to Nick, a retired doctor, we had Hazel, who was a librarian and therefore very well read, Phyllis, who was a retired English teacher, and Ethan, a retired history professor. Pappy probably had the least formal education of the group, but there was no one I'd rather have on my side in a situation requiring common sense and street smarts.

"You realize that if we continue with this conversation, we most likely never will get around to discussing the book," I warned Nick.

"Fine by me." Nick turned toward the center of the room. "Zoe is involved in another murder investigation," he announced. "How many of you are interested in finding out more about it?"

Everyone in the room agreed that they'd like to discuss the case.

"Okay, I'll tell you what I know."

After everyone took a seat, I walked the group through the highlights of the investigation to date, including the antiques auction and the series of events that took place following the auction. I left out Salinger's involvement with Barbie, as well as the names of the suspects I'd already managed to clear. By the time I was wrapping up the details of my discussion with Salinger, everyone in the room was hooked by the conversation.

"I saw Barbie on the night she died, you know," Ethan offered as he adjusted the wire-framed glasses perched on his nose. Ethan is a tall man with a thin frame and snowy white hair. Although he's new to our group, he has lived in Ashton Falls for more than ten years, having moved to the area after retiring from the university where he taught. In many ways, Ethan is a stereotypical history professor, an introvert who is more often than not distracted by whatever thoughts are stomping around in his mind. In dress he favors tweed pants topped with striped, long-sleeve dress shirts and brown corduroy jackets complete with elbow patches.

"You did? Where?"

"At the Wharf. I was there with an old colleague of mine who happened to be in town, and she came in with a man who I suppose could have been a date but looked quite a bit older than she."

"Can you describe the man?" I asked.

"I guess he was about sixty. He was maybe five ten, a little on the stocky side, with gray hair that was thinning on the top."

"Why would Barbie go out with a man so much older than she was?" Hazel asked.

"My guess is that the guy had money," Ethan offered. "His suit was designer and his watch a Rolex."

"How did you happen to notice his watch?" I had to ask.

"He raised his arm to wave over the waiter and I caught it out of the corner of my eye."

"And what time would you say that was?" I asked. Perhaps we could narrow down Barbie's movements on the night she died.

"I guess around nine. We were just finishing up and left shortly after the couple arrived. The place was packed, and the only reason I even noticed them was because the dress Barbie had on was designed to be noticed, if you know what I mean."

I did.

"Do we think this man had anything to do with Barbie's death?" Phyllis asked.

"Probably not, but I'd like to know who the guy was," I answered.

"I suppose you can check with the wait staff at the Wharf," Pappy said. "The man most likely paid with a credit card, and if Barbie was dressed in the manner described, I imagine the server remembered her. He might even have known her or known of her. Most people in town did, in spite of the fact that she didn't live here all that long."

"She certainly was one to be noticed," Nick agreed.

I looked at my watch. The Wharf closed early on weeknights until after Memorial Day, when they switched to their summer hours. Chances were that the weekend staff wouldn't be working on a Thursday anyway. I realized that following up with the wait staff was a good idea, but I supposed it would have to wait until tomorrow. The restaurant didn't open until four, but I'd probably find someone on-site several hours before that. I'd promised to help set up the kiddie carnival and food vendors the next day, but I was certain I could get away long enough to see if I could find out the identity of Barbie's date.

"You know," Ethan added, "now that I'm thinking about it, Ryder Westlake stopped by the table and chatted for a few minutes. He might know who the man was."

"Dr. Ryder Westlake?" I asked. Dr. Westlake is fairly new to the area. He's young, single, and gorgeous, so I imagine that like every other Ashtonite with a y chromosome and a pulse, he'd noticed Barbie, but I was surprised he knew her well enough to stop by her table to speak to her.

"It looked like he was on a date with the new science teacher at the high school," Ethan informed us.

"Seems rude to stop to talk to Barbie if he was on a date," I commented.

"Ryder and I are pretty tight," Nick offered. "How about I call him to see what he knows?"

I watched the other members of the group as Nick spoke to Dr. Westlake. Pappy was seated next to Hazel, and the two appeared to be engaged in a private conversation. The pair made a handsome couple, if they were indeed a couple. Both were tall and thin. Pappy's hair was white, whereas Hazel's was still a rich brown. Both tended toward neatness and simplicity in style and appearance. Phyllis and Lilly were chatting about something that made them laugh at regular intervals, while Ethan appeared lost in thought.

I decided to use the time to check on Charlie, who was outdoors with the other dogs. In all, the current book club members own five dogs among us. When Charlie saw me, he trotted over to greet me. I talked to him for a few minutes, then sent him back to his friends, thinking Nick had probably concluded his conversation by then.

"The man's name is Pinkerton Lowell," Nick informed us. "He's an art dealer from San Francisco. Ryder said the two weren't good friends but had met at an art auction a while back. He stopped to say hi when he recognized him but didn't take the time to chat and was uncertain as to his exact reason for being in Ashton Falls."

"The fact that Barbie was seen at an auction the weekend before her death and that she was having dinner with an art dealer tracks," I pointed out. "I'm even more convinced than I was before that her death had something to do with the auction."

"You think this man killed her?" Lilly asked.

"Probably not," I admitted.

"I think we should discuss the book," Phyllis said. "This is a book club, and I did take the time to read it."

"Let's take a short break to refill our drinks and then segue into the book discussion," Hazel suggested.

"Actually," I stood up, "I think I'm going to go. I appreciate your help with the case, but I'm pretty tired and it's going to be a long weekend."

"Of course, dear," Hazel responded. "We'll see you tomorrow at the park."

Chapter 15

Friday, May 24

By the time I got to the Zoo the next morning, Goliath was doing much better. He was up and about and as cranky as a caged mountain lion should be. Scott gave us the go-ahead to start administering his medications through his food, which allowed us to back off the sedatives considerably. It makes my heart glad when I know that in some small way we've been instrumental in giving one of Mother Nature's children a second chance at life. It's days like this one that really bring home the importance of what we do.

"It looks like we're back on track." Jeremy walked up to stand next to me as I watched Goliath pacing to and fro from a vantage point just outside his cage.

"It was touch and go for a while, but it looks like the big guy will be okay," I agreed. "I have a feeling it's going to be a good day."

"Do you feel better after your day off?"

"Much. It's a good thing too, with the busy weekend we have planned. I need to get over to the park to check on things for the kiddie carnival, but I wanted to check in with you first. Is everything set for the pet adoption tomorrow?"

"We're good to go," Jeremy assured me. "Tiffany is going to hold down the fort here while you and I are at the park. It looks like we only have six dogs, eight puppies, three cats, and nine kittens to place.

Puppies and kittens tend to go fast, so I'm betting we'll be done by noon tomorrow."

"That'd be fine by me. I have the kiddie carnival to monitor, and Zak said something about bringing Scooter over to enjoy the festivities."

"How's Zak doing with Scooter?"

"Really good, actually. I think even he was surprised at what a natural he is in the parenting department. They spent the day together yesterday. Zak bought him a bunch of new clothes and they did guy stuff like skeet shooting and miniature golf. Scooter was still sleeping like a baby when I stopped by Zak's this morning."

"I can't imagine spending an entire day with the human tornado."

"I think we might have seen the last of the tornado. He's been really pleasant after that first horrible night. I don't think Scooter is a bad kid, I just think he's been lonely since his mom died. Spending time with Zak has been really good for him. Hopefully, the good behavior will continue once his dad gets back."

"Maybe Zak can continue to hang out with Scooter. Like a mentor or something."

"Yeah, he mentioned something like that. Are you bringing Morgan to the park today?"

"Probably not. She *is* only a month old, so I don't think she'll care about the events, and I worry about exposing her to all those germs."

"I think she'd enjoy the colors and lights. Mom and Dad are bringing Harper for a while. If you get the chance, you should strap her into her baby pack and bring her by."

"Maybe. Are you leaving now?"

"Yeah. I need to make sure everyone who was supposed to show up actually did. I'll be on my cell. Call if you need me."

The park was located at the edge of town and was designed so that the focal point was a gazebo strategically placed smack dab in the center of a large grassy area. The plan for the weekend was to use the gazebo for musical events, as well as announcements and event judging. The kiddie carnival, which consisted of vendors offering games such as the ring toss, was set up on one side of the gazebo, while the craft fair, where home-crafted items were on sale, was set up on the opposite side. Food vendors congregated near the picnic area, allowing visitors to use the tables provided to eat their meals. Because the main attraction on this particular weekend was the lake and the beach, additional food carts were set up along the pier. Most of the water events were scheduled to take place on Saturday and Sunday. In addition to the kiddie carnival, which opened at three, the main draw for today was the beer crawl, which was an adults-only event held later in the evening.

By the look of things, most of the individuals and organizations sponsoring booths had shown up early and construction of the temporary structures was well underway.

"How are we doing?" I asked Willa, who was seated at a card table with a clipboard and ID badges.

"Pretty good. About three-quarters of the individuals who signed up to have booths have arrived. I'm sure the others will be here shortly. So far no one has called to cancel."

"How can I help?" I asked.

"Tawny might need help getting the ticket booth assembled. We decided to place it just to the left of the park entrance."

"Okay, I'm on it. Let me know if anything else comes up."

There was a delicious feeling of excitement and expectation in the air as I made my way across the grass toward Main Street. Ashton Falls is a town known for its festivals and events, and at times the constant cycles of planning and implementation can become overwhelming, but on days like this, when the sun is shining and the sky is blue, I wouldn't want to be anywhere else. Ashton Falls might be a small town with zero nightlife, a limited budget, and an active gossip hotline—not everyone's cup of tea, I'm sure—but to me, it's home.

"I'm here to help," I announced to Tawny, a single mom who runs a preschool and afterschool day care in order to pay the bills and still be around for her kids.

"Fantastic." Tawny smiled. "When Willa asked me to do this, I figured how hard could it be? What I didn't know was that one would need a degree in engineering to figure out these directions. How can I slip slot A into groove B when I have no idea where either slot A or groove B is located?"

I looked at the pile of pieces, which appeared random at best. "Maybe this is slot A?"

"Maybe, but what slot is the one over here?" Tawny held up what looked to be an identical piece.

I shrugged. "It looks like it fits. Let's try it and see what happens."

After five false starts, Tawny and I figured out which peg went in which hole and started to erect the structure. I just hoped the whole thing wouldn't come crashing down midway through the day.

"Need some help?" Levi asked a short time later as I struggled to erect one of the preformed walls of the shack we used for outdoor events.

"I'd love it."

"They sent you to do this on your own?" Levi asked.

"Tawny was helping, but she got called away."

Levi grabbed one end of the wall while I grabbed the other. We lifted it until it was flush with the adjoining wall. I held it in place while Levi installed the bolts.

"You look better," I commented as we worked. "Did you get some sleep?"

"I did. It was the first time I'd really been able to sleep since I found out about Barbie. Where's Zak?" Levi asked.

"He's at home. Scooter was wiped out after his long day yesterday. Zak's going to bring him over once he wakes up."

"Did you talk to Salinger yesterday?"

"Yeah. He's going to see if he can track down lifeguard guy, now that we have a pretty good photo to use as a way of identifying him. He's also going to check with the auction house to see what he can find out about the painting. I thought I'd stop by after I finish here to see if he has any news."

"I think that should do it." Levi took a step back. I held my breath, but the structure we'd erected didn't fall over, as I'd feared.

"Yay us. I guess we should find Willa and get our next assignment."

Levi and I gathered the tools we'd been using and started back toward the check-in table, where Willa was still holding court.

"How was book club?" Levi asked as we walked through the park.

"We never did get around to discussing the book, at least not before I left. But I did find out that Barbie had dinner with an art dealer on the night she died."

"Art dealer?" Levi stopped walking.

"Ryder Westlake was at the Wharf and ran into them. Nick said that according to Ryder, the man is an art dealer from San Francisco. I was going to bring it up to Salinger when I saw him."

"Do we have a name for this guy?" Levi wondered.

"Pinkerton Lowell. Dr. Westlake didn't really have a conversation with the man, so he didn't know why he was in town, how he knew Barbie, or what business they might have together."

"Maybe we should have a chat with him," Levi suggested.

"As far as I know, he's left the area, and I don't have his contact information. I thought I'd just let Salinger follow up on it. Following up on leads is his job, and to be honest, I have a full day ahead of me."

"Pinkerton Lowell isn't a common name," Levi pointed out. "We know he's an art dealer and we know he lives in San Francisco. How hard could it be to come up with a telephone number?"

I sighed. I really did have a lot to do and would have preferred to let Salinger call the guy. I suppose this was my fault for mentioning anything to Levi. I knew he wasn't going to let it go, so I agreed to help him with a strategy for the call if he could get the number. Levi hurried off, most likely to find a computer, while I continued on toward Willa.

I was halfway back to the registration table when I noticed the dog I'd come to think of as Scamp trotting across the lawn toward Main Street. I changed direction and followed him. I lost sight of him after he ducked into the alley behind the shops on the main drag but decided to go ahead and do a sweep as long as I was there. I noticed Phillip Hayes's water truck parked in the alley behind Bertie's Clip and Curl and let myself in the back door of the popular beauty shop.

"Hey, Zoe, what brings you by?" Bertie asked from her position behind the chair where Loretta Santiago was sitting. "Did you finally decide to tame those curls?"

"No, the curls stay. I was following a medium-sized tan dog with darker-colored ears. I noticed your back door was open and thought he might have come in here."

Bertie looked around the pink and silver shop. "Don't see him."

"I saw Phillip's truck in the alley. I thought he might have seen him."

"He's in the back room switching out the water if you want to ask him."

"Thanks. I think I will."

Bertie's is what can only be referred to as the last of the old-fashioned beauty parlors. Giant hair dryers lined one wall, where women who still came in for roller sets congregated on a weekly basis to catch up and update their hairdos. I knew that the average age of Bertie's customers was just shy of seventy-three, but the women who patronized the establishment were a loyal bunch who could be counted on to show up for their weekly appointments like clockwork.

"Morning, Phillip," I greeted him.

"Hey, Zoe. Here to get your hair cut? Bet you'd look cute with a bob."

Why did everyone keep asking me that? My hair was long and thick and curly, but in spite of the fact that I hadn't changed the style since I was ten, it did seem to suit me. Or so I thought.

"No, I just popped in to look for a dog. Light brown, about so high." I held out my hand. "You seen him?"

"Sure. He's been making the rounds through town."

"I meant have you seen him in the last few minutes?"

"Oh. Then no."

"It's a terrible thing about Barbie." I decided to fish around a bit, as long as I had Phillip's attention.

"Chick was a bitch. If you ask me, she got what she deserved."

"I thought you were friends," I commented.

Phillip shrugged. "Not sure why you thought that."

"Yeah, I hear you. Barbie wasn't my favorite human on the planet either, but it was a shame to ruin those shoes."

Phillip laughed. "Have you ever seen anything so ridiculous? No wonder she tripped."

"Yeah." I tried for casual rather than alert. "She must have been toasted."

"Toasted is right. Me, I prefer a sensible girl who wears sensible shoes. Like you." Phillip leered at me.

Eww. I figured I'd lure him into a conversation by pretending to feel nothing but disdain for Barbie, but I certainly didn't want to end up with a date.

I leaned in close. "You know," I whispered like a coconspirator, "I heard she was out with a man twice her age that night."

"Yeah, she had dinner with the old man, but as soon as they were done she dumped him. Even Barbie is more discriminating than to nail some guy who needs little blue pills to do the deed."

"So you saw her after she left the restaurant?"

Phillip took a step back, then looked directly at me. "Not really," he answered. "I was at the restaurant having dinner with my wife. We left at the same time. I saw the old guy leave in a limo while Barbie took off on foot."

I did remember someone saying that Phillip and his wife had gone sailing and then had had dinner at the Wharf. That must be how he knew about the shoes. Dang; I'd thought I was on to something.

"Well, I guess I should get going," I said.

"Yeah, me too. I'll see you around."

Not if I see you first.

After leaving Bertie's, I went back to the park and the registration booth I'd been heading toward before I spotted Scamp.

"Oh, good, you came back." Willa sounded relieved.

"The ticket booth is erected and ready to go," I reported.

"Excellent. Why don't you go help Ellie set up the main food trailer? She was here a while ago but seemed out of sorts."

"Okay, I'm on it."

When I found Ellie, I could see right off what Willa had been referring to. Ellie not only was less than her jovial self but it looked like she'd been crying.

"What's wrong?" I asked as I wrapped her in a best-friend hug.

"Rob and Hannah had to fly back to Maine to visit his dad," Ellie informed me. "He's been sick for a while, but I guess he's taken a turn for the worse, so they had to leave right away."

"Oh, Ellie, I'm so sorry."

"I'm not sure why I fell apart the way I did. I knew Rob planned to make the trip at some point, but it all happened so quickly that I guess I didn't have time to prepare. When I kissed Hannah good-bye this morning, I just started bawling and couldn't stop. Rob said they could be gone for several weeks, depending on how things go."

"Several weeks is a long time to be away from your fiancé," I sympathized.

Ellie looked startled by my comment. "Yeah, it is. The good news is that we decided to get married right away after they get back. We decided on June 28th. I called Zak, and we're all set on using his friend's house in Hawaii beginning on June 29th."

"Wow, that's really soon. It'll be hard to get everything together before then."

"Rob said it would be easier to take one long leave from work rather than taking a leave now to go to his parents, go back to work for a month, and then take off again for a wedding. We decided to do something small and simple. It'll probably just be my mom and you and Zak and Levi. I suppose I should invite Jeremy and Kelly as well."

"Are you sure?" I looked Ellie in the eye. "You only get married once."

"Yeah, I know, but honestly, I just want the whole thing behind me so I can finally be Hannah's real mom and not just her dad's girlfriend."

Ellie returned to her task of unloading and sorting groceries and I joined in to help her. Our conversation had made me more uncomfortable than I'd been for a long time. Ellie was upset that Hannah was leaving but didn't seem at all concerned that Rob was likewise going to be gone. And she was focused on being Hannah's mother but didn't seem overly excited about being Rob's wife. I loved Ellie and didn't want her to make what sounded like it could very well be the worst decision of her life. I almost blurted out my feelings on the subject, but sanity checked in at the last minute, and I realized that it might be better to wait for a more opportune time.

"What part of Maine is Rob from?" I asked.

"Bangor. It seems like it would be a pretty part of the country to see. I was sorry things happened so quickly and I was unable to go with them."

"I'm sure he'll take you to meet his family once his father . . ." I started to say *dies*, but that sounded really cold.

"Yeah, I guess he hadn't been back since he moved to Ashton Falls. He seemed really nervous about the whole thing. I'm not sure why. He gets along okay with his family, as far as I can tell."

"True, but if his dad is as sick as it seems, I'm sure the whole thing is very stressful. It's probably best that you didn't go along this time. That way he can focus on his dad."

"Yeah, I guess. I sure am going to miss Hannah, though. I was really looking forward to bringing her to the kiddie carnival this weekend."

"There's always next year." I know my attempt at comforting my best friend was completely lame, but I couldn't think of anything to say, given the circumstances.

Ellie stopped what she was doing and looked out across the park. "I thought Levi would be here."

"He was," I informed her. "He helped me set up the ticket booth, and then I made the mistake of informing him that Ethan saw Barbie having dinner with an art dealer from San Francisco on the night she died. He took off to see if he could track down the man's contact information."

"Poor Levi. He's really taking this hard."

"Yes, he is," I agreed.

"Do you think this art dealer had anything to do with Barbie's death?" Ellie asked.

I stopped to consider her question. On one hand, my initial impression was that he most likely didn't have anything to do with it. Still, he'd been having dinner with her at nine. Salinger had said that the TOD was between eleven and one, and Ethan had told us that they'd just arrived as he was getting ready to leave, which meant they were probably at the restaurant until 10:30. We also knew that Barbie was caught trying to steal an antique clock, and that the lot number on the flyer she left for Levi was assigned to a painting. Maybe this art dealer was our killer.

"Zoe?" Ellie asked when I didn't respond.

"Sorry. I was thinking about your question. Yeah, I think it's very possible that this art dealer was involved in Barbie's death. I'm just not sure why he would kill her."

"If he's guilty and you ask him about it, he won't tell you anything," Ellie logically stated. "It might be better not to let him know you're on to him if you do think he's involved."

"True."

"Maybe Zak can use his magic computer to find out more about the guy."

"That's a good idea. I'll call him."

"Oh, look." Ellie was gazing past my shoulder after I'd hung up with Zak, who'd promised to see what he could find out. "There's your mom and dad with Harper."

I turned and waved as my family approached. Harper might be a little young to really enjoy the kiddie carnival, but her big sister was going to get a photo of her first Memorial Day event anyway. "Take a photo of Harper and me?" I handed Ellie my phone.

"Sure." Ellie teared up.

Good going, Zoe. Make your best friend cry.

"I'm sure Dad can do it if you'd rather not."

"No. It's okay." Ellie wiped her eyes. "I want to."

Ellie snapped a photo of Harper and me in front of the carousel, which I was certain would be hanging on my wall for the rest of my life. She really is the most perfect baby. I'm still not certain about my future as a mother of a member or members of the next generation, but as I looked at the photo of me holding my baby sister, I realized it was possible that eventuality wasn't as impossible as it once had seemed.

"What are your plans for the rest of the day?" I asked my parents after I returned Harper to their care.

"We thought we'd walk around a bit. Maybe have some lunch. And then probably return home so Harper can have a proper nap," my dad answered. "You should come by later, if you have a chance. We're making tri tip for dinner."

"I have the beer crawl tonight," I reminded him. "At least, I think Zak and I are still doing that. I haven't talked to him about it since he's been sitting for Scooter."

"How's he doing with that?" Mom asked.

"Really good. Better than I could ever have imagined. Apparently, he's as good at parenting as he is everything else."

"I never doubted it for a minute," Mom informed me.

Chapter 16

The highlight of opening day of the four-day weekend was the sailboat races at sunset. Entrants not only decorated their sails for the popular event but most participants dressed in nautically themed costumes as well. I was sitting on one of Ellie's picnic tables on the pier. Ellie was helping Kelly serve drinks and appetizers, while Levi and I chatted with Nick Benson. Zak and Scooter had joined us initially, but Scooter soon grew bored and asked to return to the kiddie carnival in the park. Zak had received a message from Scooter's dad saying that he'd be back in town the following day, so Zak was doing everything in his power today to ensure that Scooter had as much fun as a nine-year-old could.

"Looks like Ethan might win again this year," Nick commented as he shoveled one of Ellie's gourmet burgers into his mouth.

"I don't know," Levi countered. "The boat with the rainbow sail has been biding its time for the final push to the finish."

"Perhaps," Nick acknowledged. "But Ethan is familiar with the lake, giving him an advantage over someone from out of the area. I'm not much of a betting man, but if I were, my money would be on someone who knows the lake."

"Seems like this race gets bigger every year," I commented. "I miss the days when it was reserved for locals only."

"The more entrants we have, the more income we make," Levi reminded me.

"Yeah, that's true." I took a sip of my wine and watched the families on the beach as Nick and Levi discussed the latest upgrades in sailing technology. Nick had a sailboat but was disinclined to deal with the crowd the race attracted, and Levi had grown up sailing but hadn't had regular access to a boat since his dad died and his mom sold the family craft.

"Try this crab-stuffed chili relleno." Ellie set a bowl with the appetizer surrounded by sliced sourdough bread in the center of the table.

I broke off a piece of the bread and tasted the spicy dish made with crab, chili, cheese, and a wonderful red sauce. "This is really good," I complimented. "And it has just the right amount of kick to make it spicy without burning your mouth."

"Is that sour cream?" Levi asked.

"Among other things." Ellie nodded. "I'm also working on a crab martini and shrimp wontons. The process of coming up with new offerings has been fun, if nothing else."

"You can never go wrong with onion soup mix and sour cream," I contributed.

Ellie laughed. "I'll remember that."

"It looks like the leaders are about to make the final turn." Nick refocused our attention on the race. "Ethan is still in the lead, but you were right about rainbow guy closing in to establish a close second."

"The boat with the yellow sail has been gaining ground as well," I offered. I watched the various boats jockeying for position as they headed into the final leg of the race.

"Yellow sail guy is lining up all wrong for the turn," Nick said. "By the time he gets straightened out, he'll drop back at least three positions."

"Opening things up for the boat with the red, white, and blue sail," Levi speculated.

"Exactly. My prediction is Ethan in first, the boat with the rainbow sail in second, and the boat with the red, white, and blue theme in third."

"The all-woman crew in the boat with the pink and white sail are lining up to make a tight turn," I pointed out. "My money is on them for third."

"No, they don't . . ." Nick stopped speaking in midsentence. "Well, who do we have here?" he asked.

I looked away from the water to see what Nick was referring to. Scamp was not only sitting at his side but had one of his grubby paws on his lap.

"That's Scamp," I informed Nick. "He's a stray I've been trying to catch for a week. I can't believe he's just sitting here, calm as can be. He seems to like you."

"Is this the dog you were telling us about at book club?" Nick asked. "The one who molested poor Muffet?"

"One and the same. I wish I had my leash. I'd like to grab him before he takes off again."

"Oh, I don't know." Nick scratched his head. "He looks pretty content to me." Nick picked a piece of the half of hamburger he had left from his meal and fed it to Scamp, who swallowed it in one bite. "Have Ellie bring him a patty of his very own."

I waved Ellie over and put in Nick's order. I kept waiting for the other shoe to drop and Scamp to scamper away. Apparently, he must have realized that food was on the way because he lay down at Nick's feet and waited for his order to arrive.

"You say the dog is a stray?" Nick asked.

"I've already run a list of missing pets and he's not on it. I forwarded his photo to other shelters in the area but didn't have a single bite. I keep hoping I can catch the guy and bring him back to the Zoo. He's a crafty little thing. I'm betting that if I can get him cleaned up, I can find him a home."

"I'll take him," Nick offered.

"Really? That would be great."

"That is, if Scamp wants to come home with me. How about it?" he asked the little dog.

Scamp raised his head and thumped his tail on the deck.

"Since I never actually took custody of him, I don't have to require you to adopt him. If he'll go with you, I guess he's yours."

Scamp enjoyed his burger while Ethan completed the race, taking home another first-place trophy in the process. After the race was over and congratulations had been offered, I nervously watched as Nick stood up and started toward the parking lot.

"Well I'll be," I whispered as Scamp happily followed Nick to his car, and then jumped into the front seat when Nick opened the door.

"Guess the dog knows what he wants," Levi commented.

"Yeah, I guess he does. Jeremy and I have been trying to catch him all week. Every time we got close enough to nab him, he took off."

Levi shrugged. "Of course he took off. You were going to take him to doggie jail."

"First of all, he couldn't have known where I was taking him, and second, it's a very nice doggie jail."

"Jail is jail," Levi said.

"Speaking of jail . . ." I watched as Sheriff Salinger approached us from the parking area.

"What do you think he wants?" Levi wasn't a fan of the man.

"Maybe he has news," I replied, hoping Salinger was here to share with us, not interrogate us.

"I still can't believe you are working with him after what he did to you."

"You want to catch Barbie's killer," I pointed out. "Working with Salinger is our best bet at doing that. Be nice," I warned.

"Mind if I join you?" Salinger asked.

I gestured toward an empty bench across from where Levi and I were sitting, indicating that he was welcome to take it.

"I have news you might be interested in," Salinger began. "The owner of One Man's Trash regained consciousness. He identified this man as the one who shot him."

Salinger showed me a photo of a man with dark hair and eyes.

"Lifeguard guy," I confirmed.

"I don't suppose you've seen him since we spoke?"

"No. Sorry. Have you tried Googling him?"

Salinger actually smiled. "I did. Problem is that he moved out of his last known residence two months ago. Since that time he seems to have simply dropped off the grid. We have an APB out on him, but the man has gone to a lot of trouble to disappear, so I doubt we'll find him."

The fact that he went off grid two months earlier lined up with the time when Barbie had disappeared. I suspected the two of them were in cahoots on whatever it was they were into. "Did the owner of the antiques store know why the man shot him, or what might have happened to Barbie?"

"He said the man was after a painting he'd bought at the auction. At which he also bought the clock Ms. Bennington was trying to steal. The store owner didn't know why the man might want the painting since it didn't seem to have any real value, but he'd already sold it. He said the guy shot him and torched the place once he realized the painting wasn't on the premises."

"Okay. So what's the deal with the painting?" I had to wonder.

"I contacted the auction house. They had a photo of the item that was sold." Salinger handed me the photo. It was an appealing landscape with a nice color palette, but it certainly didn't look like anything worth killing over.

"Did you find out who bought it from One Man's Trash?" I asked.

"A man by the name of Pinkerton Lowell. Apparently, he's an art dealer in San Francisco."

"Pinkerton Lowell had dinner with Barbie on the night she died," I pointed out.

"I'm aware of that. I called Mr. Lowell's business and learned that he flew to Europe after leaving Ashton Falls. His assistant told me that he must have taken the painting with him since he hadn't dropped it off there. I checked with the airline and was told that he hadn't checked baggage of any type. The painting was much too large to carry on."

"So where is it?" Levi asked.

"Good question. I was hoping you might know."

"Why would I know?" Levi wondered.

"Apparently, Ms. Bennington left you a clue as to what was going on. Zoe told me about the newspaper during an earlier conversation. I was hoping there might be a clue that would point us in the direction of the artwork that seems to be behind all of this."

"The only thing I found in the post office box was the flyer with the lot number for the painting," Levi answered.

"Is there a way to get hold of this Pinkerton Lowell even if he is in Europe?" I asked.

"If he's guilty of Barbie's murder, he's most likely long gone," Levi pointed out.

"I don't think he's guilty," I said. "The owner of One Man's Trash bought the painting at the auction. We have to assume that Barbie was supposed to buy it but was unable to for some reason. Maybe she overslept or got held up in traffic or whatever. By the time she got to the auction, the painting was gone. She talks to the people at the auction house and finds out who bought it. She later breaks into the place, hoping to steal it. We have to assume that either the painting was already gone or she didn't have time to find it before she was caught."

"The painting was sold on Saturday and she wasn't caught breaking into One Man's Trash until the following Wednesday," Levi pointed out.

"Okay, so maybe she didn't find out who bought the painting right away. Maybe the people at the auction house wouldn't give her the information she wanted, so she had to get it another way."

"Or maybe the painting wasn't delivered to the store right away," Salinger supposed. "I can make a note to ask the store owner about that."

"Anyway," I added, "she must have found out that Pinkerton Lowell bought the painting from One Man's Trash, which is most likely why she was dining with him on Friday. She must have been either trying to buy it or steal it from him. She ends up dead shortly after their dinner, so it would seem that Pinkerton must be involved in some way."

"The fact that lifeguard guy broke into One Man's Trash the week following Barbie's death seems to indicate that he wasn't aware that the painting had been sold. Maybe Barbie was planning to double-cross whomever she worked for," Levi speculated.

"The painting does seem to be the key," Salinger agreed. "Perhaps if we can find it, we can unravel why it is that people are willing to kill for it."

"Maybe Barbie was successful," Levi said. "Barbie was supposed to buy the painting at the auction but failed. She tried to steal it but failed. She did, however, discover who bought it, so she decides to use her best weapon, her body, to get it back. We know Barbie and Pinkerton had dinner on Friday. Maybe the reason that Pinkerton didn't have the painting on the plane was because Barbie was successful in getting it from him."

"Okay, so why did her partner in crime break into One Man's Trash the next week?" Salinger asked.

"Maybe Barbie was planning a double-cross. Or maybe she didn't tell anyone she'd managed to get the painting," Levi added.

"But someone found out and killed her," I realized. "If her partner was still looking for the painting the week after her death, he couldn't be the one who killed her if we assume the reason she was killed is because she had the painting. That means someone *else* figured out what was going on."

"Okay, then who killed her, and where is the painting now?" Salinger asked.

"You're the cop," Levi pointed out. "Seems like that's something you should know."

Salinger frowned.

"Phillip told me that he saw Barbie leave the restaurant the night of her death," I provided. "He said she left alone on foot. He didn't mention her carrying a painting."

"So maybe she made the deal earlier and then had dinner with Pinkerton Lowell to celebrate," Levi pointed out.

"Where was she staying?" Salinger asked. "Maybe she left the painting in her room."

"No, she wouldn't do that if she was planning to double-cross whomever she was working for," I pointed out. "She'd hide it somewhere her partners wouldn't think to look."

"The cemetery," Levi said. "She'd hide it in the cemetery."

"What? Why?" I asked.

"There's a crypt in the cemetery. It's really old and hasn't been used in years. One time we," Levi paused, "visited it, and Barbie made the comment that it would be a good place to hide something."

Visited it? *Eww.* I knew what was implied.

"So let's go and check it out," Salinger said.

"I'll tell Ellie what we're doing," I offered. "She won't be done for another hour at least, so I'll arrange to meet up with her after we check out the cemetery."

The Ashton Falls Cemetery, an old establishment dating back to before the development of the town, was several miles away. The crypt Levi mentioned had been built over a hundred years earlier. It was old and starting to look a bit weathered, and as far as I could tell, no one had accessed the locked door for years. Levi reached into a crevice that was hidden by years of overgrowth. He must have pushed a lever or something because the door popped open ever so slightly. Levi pushed the door open the rest of the way, while Salinger shone his flashlight inside. It was dark and dank and dusty, not at all the type of place that would lend itself to acts of amorous affection.

Salinger balked. "I'm not going in there."

"Scared of the dark?" Levi teased.

"Claustrophobic."

"We'll go; you wait here," I suggested.

Salinger handed Levi his flashlight. Levi went in first and I followed behind.

At first I couldn't make out any details as my eyes struggled to adjust to the dark. After a few minutes, I was able to see that there were compartments carved into the walls, with wooden coffins placed inside of them. The nooks carved into the walls were just barely large enough for each coffin to be slid inside, so all that could be observed of the final resting places of those buried within the walls were the very back edges of the wooden boxes. Each box had a name and date carved into it: Harvey Johnson 1865–1926, Lillian Johnson 1842–1905.

"Wow, these are really old," I whispered. I don't know why I was whispering; it wasn't as if the residents of the crypt were going to hear me.

"Yeah, they go back a bit."

In the center of the room were two coffins, placed side by side on a stone pedestal, giving them an air of importance. I didn't know anything about the history of the place, but I was willing to bet these coffins belonged to some powerful couple, while the others buried around the room most likely belonged to family or other people associated with them.

Levi began to open the lid of one of the coffins in the center of the room.

"Levi, what are you doing?" I hissed.

"We need to look inside."

"Someone is buried in there. It seems so . . ." I searched for a word that would convey the depth of my revulsion and discomfort that Levi was about to disturb the last resting place of some long-ago human who'd lived in the area.

"Don't worry. It's empty," Levi informed me.

"Empty? How do you know that?"

I couldn't actually see Levi's coloring in the darkened room, but I was certain he was blushing. "We looked inside when Barbie and I were here before," he answered.

Levi lifted the lid, then shone the light into the interior of the box and lifted out the painting that had caused such a stir. It was probably about three feet by three feet in size, unframed, and appeared to have been painted by a talented if not overly original artist. Levi handed it to me as he replaced the lid.

"Let's get out of here," I whispered.

"Yeah, okay." Levi took one last look around before we returned to the entrance of the room, where Salinger was waiting. We closed the door to the crypt, being careful to make sure it latched, and followed the sheriff back to his office.

"What now?" I asked as Levi and I sat across from Salinger, who was sitting behind his desk.

"I guess we get an art specialist to tell us what all the fuss is about," Salinger said.

"Are there any of those in Ashton Falls?" I wondered.

"Doubtful," Salinger admitted. "I'll call the Bryton Lake office and have them send someone up. I'm sure it will be at least a day or two before anyone gets here. I'll lock this up in the evidence room in the meantime. Maybe we can get some prints off it as well."

"You'll call us when you hear anything?"

"Yeah, I'll call."

Chapter 17

Saturday, May 25

The water-sports demonstration was held in midmorning, while the lake was still free of waves from recreational boats. Even though we hadn't had much time to practice, Levi and I rocked the show with simultaneous gun barrels across the wake. We'd been skiing and boarding together since we were kids, so we enjoyed a natural rhythm others would need hours of concentrated practice to duplicate. After the competition, I needed to hurry back to the park for the pet adoption clinic, so I arranged to meet up with Zak later in the day, after he'd taken Scooter home to his father.

"Good turn out," Jeremy commented as droves of spectators wandered among the rows of animal cages.

"Yeah," I agreed. "We've already collected over twenty apps. Most of them look like good prospects. We're going to be busy processing everyone."

"We have nine applications from locals who want to take their pet home today. I think they all meet our criteria, and since we know them, I figured we could skip the background checks. I told them to come back in a couple of hours." Jeremy handed me the stack of applications.

I looked through them. Most wanted puppies; a few wanted kittens. "Yeah, they look good. Go ahead and make the arrangements. Any others we need to deal with right away?"

"Most of the other applications are from visitors from out of the area who are more than happy to pick their pets up on their way out of town tomorrow afternoon, but there was one application from a man interested in Juniper. He said he'd only be in town for the day."

Juniper was a Great Dane mix who weighed over 175 pounds. He was not only a large animal but had an abundance of energy as well. We'd need just the right placement for this high-maintenance dog. I considered the application. The man lived on a ten-acre parcel in the valley. He was a retired firefighter who now worked as a freelance writer, single, and lived alone, and his last dog had passed away three months earlier. He listed five references, including a veterinarian in the valley who I'd met on a couple of occasions.

"Go ahead and call this veterinarian. I've met him a few times and he seems like a good guy. If he'll vouch for the guy, go ahead and arrange for the adoption."

"Okay, fantastic. The guy seemed to really want to take Juniper home today."

"It looks like Rosalie is fixated on that little black kitten," I said, referring to Jeremy's former neighbor, a five-year-old who had moved to the area with her mother, Jessica, the month before. "Too bad she can't have a pet in the apartment complex where they live."

"I've been sitting here for the past half hour watching her. I'm actually considering adopting the kitten myself. Jessica and Rosalie babysit for Morgan several times a week. She can play with her when she's at my place."

"If you want to do that, you'd better stick an ADOPTED sign on the cage. I've noticed several other people who have an eye on her."

Jeremy hesitated briefly. "I suppose I should ask Phyllis about it." Jeremy had rented Phyllis King's condo. "She was fine with my having Squeaky, but a kitten is another thing."

"Put the ADOPTED sign on the kitten so no one else snaps her up and call Phyllis. If I know Phyllis, and I do, she'll be fine with it."

"Okay." Jeremy smiled. "I'll do it. Rosalie will be so excited."

By the time midafternoon rolled around, most of the animals had either been adopted or had adoption applications pending. It looked like the Zoo was going to be quiet the upcoming week, although experience had taught me that as soon as we moved them out, new animals needing homes moved in. Spring and early summer was our busiest time for puppies and kittens. Every puppy or kitten owner who dropped off a litter was given a certificate for a free spay for their pet and strongly encouraged to use it. Most did, but a few pet owners continued to bring litter after litter to us.

"You going to the arts and music festival?" Jeremy asked as we began cleaning up.

"Yeah. Zak should be back from dropping off Scooter in a half hour or so. I thought we'd check it out before we're supposed to meet up with Levi and Ellie later this evening."

"I heard they had some good bands this year. I might go pick up Morgan from the sitter and bring her back over. You were right about her liking the lights and commotion."

"Yeah, there are a lot of new sights, smells, and sounds for a baby to check out. Mom said Harper was really interested in everything for about an hour and then became overly stimulated and fussy."

"Same thing happened to Morgan yesterday, although I think she'll really like the music. Anytime I can't get her to sleep, I sing to her. She really seems to enjoy the sound of my guitar."

"Did you get hold of Phyllis?"

"I did, and she was fine with me adopting Fred."

"She already has a name?"

"Rosalie's idea."

"You'd better make sure Fred and Squeaky aren't left alone unless Squeaky is in his cage. Somehow I can see Fred deciding he'd be a fun play toy."

"Don't worry, I'll keep them apart. I had both a hamster and a cat when I was growing up and it worked out okay."

"Yes, but Fred is a kitten and much more likely to want to play with the little guy."

"True."

"Will you bring Jessica and Rosalie with you if you come back for the music festival?"

"I plan to ask them, although I'm betting Rosalie will want to stay at my place to play with Fred. Now that I think about it, maybe I should stay home and supervise."

"You can always take Fred to the Zoo and pick her up later," I suggested.

Jeremy glanced toward where Rosalie was sitting next to Fred's cage. "I don't think Rosalie will go for that. I can always catch the music festival next year. Maybe Morgan and I will BBQ for Jessica and

Rosalie at my place instead of coming back into town."

I smiled at my assistant. I couldn't believe how much he'd changed since he'd become a dad. The old Jeremy would never have chosen to miss an opportunity to hang out, drink beer, and listen to jazz. Although he was only twenty-one, he was a lot more settled than many of my friends who were a good ten years older.

Walking hand in hand with Zak at the arts and music festival was the most fun I'd had in a long time. The sun on my bare shoulders felt wonderful, and the fantastic food offerings, paired with beer tasting from many fine breweries, left me feeling relaxed and mellow. Having him spend time with Scooter appeared to have been really good for both of them, but I had to admit I was happy to have Zak back to myself for a while. I hadn't wanted to intrude on the guy time Zak and Scooter shared, so other than a meal here and there, I'd spent very little time with him for almost a week.

"I haven't heard this band before," Zak commented as we sat on a bench under a tree.

"They're new this year," I said as I nibbled on a deep fried prawn I'd dipped in the best cocktail sauce I'd ever tasted. "They have a unique sound I really like."

"Would you like another glass of beer?" Zak asked, noticing that my glass was empty.

"Yeah, but not right now. I thought we'd listen to the music for a while and then walk around a bit more. There are a couple of new breweries I want to check out."

"I thought Levi and Ellie would be here by now."

I laid my head on his shoulder as we continued to listen to the music. "Ellie decided to work since Rob and Hannah weren't here. She mentioned meeting us at the Beach Hut at around seven. I have no idea where Levi is today. He's really focused on this investigation. It looks like we've figured out most of what was going on, but there are still a few missing pieces. I think that's making him kind of nuts."

"Have you talked to Salinger today?" Zak asked.

"No, although I half-expected him to come by looking for me. There's definitely something going on here that can't be explained by the painting everyone seems to have been after."

Zak looked at his phone and frowned.

"What's wrong?" I asked.

"It's a text from Scooter. I gave him my number and told him he could text me any time."

"He has a phone?"

"I bought him one when we went shopping. I really hope things get better with his dad, but I hated to send him home not knowing how the guy will behave once they're together again."

"Has his father been abusive?" I asked.

"Not so much abusive as neglectful. The text I just received is asking if I can meet him over near the elementary school. He says it's important."

"Go ahead. I'll head over to Ellie's. Meet me there when you're done. I'll see if I can find Levi as well, and the four of us can hang out tonight. Maybe we can have a nice dinner."

I decided to stop by Salinger's office on my way over to Ellie's. I doubted he had any news, but I was curious about the painting and why anyone would be willing to kill for it. It wasn't unpleasant, but it appeared to be pretty common, not that I'm an art expert. I'd parked my truck near where the pet adoption had been held, so I decided to walk the half mile or so to the sheriff's office.

I was turning onto Main Street when I noticed Phillip Hayes ducking into the yoga studio. I didn't realize Phillip delivered water on the weekend, but I knew Serenity offered classes on Saturdays, so maybe they'd worked something out.

The receptionist at the sheriff's office informed me that Salinger was on patrol at the arts and music festival. I should have realized he'd be there with the large influx of out-of-town guests. I asked her if she could radio him to arrange a place for us to meet. After several attempts to contact him, we finally were able to arrange a meeting at the kiddie carnival in twenty minutes.

As I walked back through town, I saw that Phillip's van was still in front of the yoga studio. It had been more than twenty minutes since I'd passed by, so perhaps he wasn't there to deliver water after all. Phillip and Serenity? Nah. Serenity could do better and besides, I'm sure she would consider hooking up with a married man to be a karma killer. Serenity paid more attention to things like karma and auras than anyone I'd ever met.

As arranged, Salinger was waiting for me near the fishing booth. I waved to him as I approached, and he indicated that I should follow him over to one of the empty benches at the food court.

"So what can I do for you?" he asked.

"I mostly just wanted to find out if you had any news on the painting."

"Actually, I do," Salinger informed me. "Let's walk while we talk. I really should be patrolling, and what I have to tell you is sensitive, so I wouldn't want anyone to overhear our conversation.'

"Yeah, okay." I stood up and followed Salinger as he walked toward the bandstand, where a new band was starting up.

"I called the Bryton Lake office when I returned from retrieving the painting yesterday. As expected, they informed me that they wouldn't be able to send anyone out to look at it for at least a week. The woman who cleans our offices overheard the conversation and informed me that one of the panelist who had been recruited to judge the art show worked in a museum. She suggested that he might be able to look at the painting. I contacted the man, who was happy to cooperate. As we thought, he said the painting, while pleasant, is nothing spectacular. He initially said he had no idea why anyone would kill for it, but after examining it more closely, he noticed that the frame looked quite old. He theorized that there might be a painting beneath the landscape. To make a long story short, when we removed the canvas from the frame, we found another canvas beneath the landscape. The man informed me that the hidden painting had been part of a collection that was stolen eight months ago. It's worth millions."

"Wow."

"Wow is right. We're still putting all the pieces together, but it looks like Ms. Bennington worked for a gang who fences stolen property. The stolen items are hidden inside or behind ordinary ones, which are then offered for sale at auctions. It appears it was Ms. Bennington's job to buy the pieces and then deliver them to the buyers. As we suspected, it looks like she was supposed to buy the painting, but it was sold to the owner of One Man's Trash before she was able to complete the transaction. She tried to steal it back, but I caught her."

"What about Pinkerton Lowell?" I asked as we circled back around to the kiddie carnival. "Was he involved in some way?"

"Not as far as we can tell. I did manage to have a telephone conversation with him. He told me that he saw the painting in One Man's Trash while he was browsing. Something about it caught his eye, so he bought it. When Ms. Bennington tracked him down and explained that she was an art buyer who was supposed to secure it for a client, he gladly sold it to her. She was grateful and agreed to have dinner with him. He says he left town later that evening."

"So he didn't know about the hidden painting?"

"He says he didn't," Salinger informed me. "He said he bought the painting on a whim but didn't really look at it all that closely. I'm not sure I believe him. If he's an art dealer, you'd think he'd notice something like a mediocre painting in a valuable frame, although I guess at this point there's no way to prove that one way or another."

"Okay, so Barbie buys the painting from the man, hides it in the cemetery, and then has dinner with Mr. Lowell. Phillip Hayes told me that he saw her leave on foot. So who killed her?"

"At first I thought it might be her partner, the man you refer to as lifeguard guy. It made sense that if he knew about Barbie's plan to keep the painting, he might have taken care of her. However, if he knew what was going on, he wouldn't have killed her until she revealed the location of the painting, and he wouldn't have bothered to break into One Man's Trash looking for it."

"So if the person or persons she worked for didn't kill her, we're back to square one," I realized.

"I'd say we are," Salinger agreed. "If you figure anything out, let me know."

"Yeah, I will," I agreed.

"And Zoe . . ."

"Yeah?"

"Don't try to be a hero. If you figure out who did it, call me."

"Yeah," I repeated. "I will."

Chapter 18

Once again, I headed toward Ellie's. The others probably were already there and worried about me. I called Zak's number, but it went to voice mail, so I left a message, telling him that I was on my way. I was crossing the park near the parking lot where I'd left my truck when it occurred to me that I really should go home to check on Charlie. Zak had brought him to the park with him earlier in the day, but he'd been home alone a good six hours by now. It made sense to change out of my Zoe's Zoo polo shirt before meeting the others for the evening anyway. I called Zak's number again and left a second message.

As I headed down Main Street, I noticed Phillip coming out of Serenity's yoga studio. He wasn't in his uniform or carrying empties, so I had to assume he was there for some reason other than delivering water. It occurred to me that he might know something about Barbie's death even if he wasn't aware of it. If he'd seen Barbie leaving the Wharf on foot, perhaps he'd noticed someone following her.

"Hey, Phillip." I pulled my truck up alongside his.

"What's up, Zoe?"

"I'm still investigating Barbie's murder, and it occurred to me that if you saw Barbie leave the Wharf on foot, maybe you saw someone following her. It seems like she died shortly after she left the place."

"Sorry," Phillip answered a bit too quickly. "I didn't see a thing."

"Yeah, well, it was worth a try." I put my truck in park and got out. "I guess as long as I'm here, I'll talk to Serenity one more time."

"She's not here," Phillip told me.

"She's not? Who were you visiting then?"

Phillip looked around. It was getting dark by this point, and most people had either gone indoors or gravitated toward the lights provided in the park. I began to get that not-so-pleasant feeling that there might be more going on than met the eye.

"I was talking to Serenity, but she left just before you got here," Phillip tried.

"Left? Why would she leave if you were still here?"

"One of the water dispensers is leaking. I told her I'd take a look and pull the door closed behind me when I was done."

"Why didn't you look at it when you first got here?" I unwisely asked.

"I did just get here. Right before you drove up. Serenity was on her way out, we chatted for a few minutes, and she told me about the water dispenser."

"I see."

I can only assume that the look of doubt on my face was obvious because the next thing I knew, Phillip had grabbed me by my hair and pulled me toward the building. He opened the door, which hadn't been closed all the way, and shoved me inside. I tried to scream, but I was so surprised by his move that by the time I realized a scream could be helpful, I was already inside.

"What the . . ."

"You just can't leave things alone, can you? Oh no, you always have to butt into things that are none of your business."

"You drugged Barbie," I accused. I actually didn't know this for certain, but somehow I'd known deep in my gut that Phillip was the guilty party all along.

"The little slut. Strutting her stuff around, flirting with me when she had no intention of following through with her little taunts. She got what she deserved."

"She was a tease, so you drugged her and pushed her off the pier?"

"No," Phillip admitted. "That was an accident. When I saw her at the restaurant with that old man, I lost it. I took my wife home and then told her that I'd forgotten my credit card at the restaurant and had to go back for it. I'm not sure why I went back, but Barbie had gotten me all worked up and I knew I needed to take care of things one way or another. Luck was on my side and she was just leaving when I got there. She kissed the grandpa she was with goodbye and set off on foot. I offered her a ride, which she accepted. Then I suggested we go somewhere for a drink, and for some reason even I don't understand, she accepted. I thought we might actually get together. I mean, she's been with every other man in town, so why not me? I mentioned getting a motel room and she laughed. When she went into the ladies' room, I slipped the drug into her drink. I figured if she wasn't going to give up what was rightfully mine, I'd take it."

"You were going to rape her."

"Yeah, so? She deserved it after all the times she flaunted herself only to tell me to piss off."

"So what happened?"

"When we left the bar, I tried to get her into the truck, but she refused. There were people around, so I couldn't force her. I followed her to the pier. I have no idea why she walked out to the end. I tried to grab her, but she pulled away and fell. Or maybe she tripped. I'm not sure, I just know that she ended up in the water."

"So why didn't you go in after her?"

Phillip shrugged. "It was cold. I didn't know she'd drown. I called her a few choice names and then left."

"What you did was wrong, and I'm sure there are consequences for drugging someone, but it sounds like Barbie's death was an accident. You need to tell someone. Salinger. We need to call him and explain everything."

"We aren't calling anyone," Phillip insisted. "No way I'm going to jail for what happened to that little slut."

"He's going to find out," I tried to reason. "It really is best that you turn yourself in."

"He's not going to find out."

I got a queasy feeling in my stomach. He'd told me everything but had no intention of turning himself in. That meant . . .

"What are you going to do?" I asked.

"What I need to."

I looked around for a way to escape, but Phillip was standing between me and the door.

"Where is Serenity?" I realized that there was no way Serenity simply left Phillip on the premises.

"The bitch is no better than her friend," Phillip answered, totally ignoring my question. His eyes had a crazed look. "I saw the light on in the studio when I was heading back after doing my rounds. I decided to stop by for a chat with the pretty lady who has been coming onto me for months."

"You think she's been coming onto you?" The guy had totally lost his mind.

"I not only think it, I know it. I've seen the way she looks at me. She's hungry for what only a real man like me can give her. She knows it and I know it."

"So where is she?"

"When I suggested that perhaps we could get together, she actually laughed in my face. Can you believe that?"

Phillip's face was turning red. I actually suspected that steam might start pouring out of his ears at any moment.

"You didn't hurt her?"

I got a sickening feeling when Phillip just smiled at me with the creepiest look I'd ever seen.

"I really think I should go." I tried to inch toward the door.

"Not so fast." He grabbed my arm.

"It's been a really long day." I tried not to panic.

Phillip pulled me toward him and tried to smell my hair. My hair! Do you have any idea how disturbing it is to have some random guy smell your hair? I lifted my leg to knee him in the groin and that, I'm afraid, is the last thing I remember.

Chapter 19

Saturday, June 21

"The past month has been the worst in the history of all months." Ellie sobbed into Levi's shoulder.

"I know, honey." Levi hugged Ellie like he was never going to let her go.

"I can't believe what's happened," Zak added. "I did everything I could. I kept thinking if I threw enough love and money at the situation, it would all work out, but I guess sometimes there are things that even money can't fix."

"I keep thinking we'll all wake up and find the past month has been a horrible dream," Levi said.

I watched my friends from above. I felt helpless to comfort them. They were all in so much pain, and I was powerless in my campaign to alleviate their grief. Life isn't always fair. I watched my friends and knew with a certainty that I'd never felt before that sometimes bad things happen to good people.

"I don't know how I'm going to make it through this," Ellie sobbed. "My heart feels like someone has reached into my chest and ripped it out. I love her so much; I don't know how I'm going to live without her."

"I know." Levi sat down on the sofa, pulling Ellie into his lap. "I know it's almost unbearable right now, but it will get better."

"Better?" Ellie sobbed. "How can it ever be better?"

Zak sat down on the sofa next to Ellie. Charlie put a paw on his knee in a show of comfort. Zak picked Charlie up and buried his face in his fur. I suspected that he'd shed a few tears, but I was certain he'd never show his grief to the others. Zak was always the strong one, the one who held everything together when the world was falling apart. "You know that we'll all get past this," he offered my two best friends.

Ellie looked at Zak. "I'm so sorry. I've been so wrapped up in my own stuff that I've barely offered my condolences to you for your own loss. I know how hard this must be for you."

I felt tears running down my face. It really had been the worst month in the history of all months. I knew in my heart that I needed to help them. I had no words or flashes of insight. Sometimes life gives you a gift only to demand a tribute in return.

"Where's Zoe?" Ellie asked.

"Right here," I said as I came down the stairs from my loft. I opened my arms and Ellie got up off of Levi's lap and walked into them. In the month since Zak had found Serenity and me unconscious on the floor of her studio, so many heartbreaking things had happened.

Serenity had suffered a blow to the head much more serious than mine and was still in a coma. It was unknown whether she'd ever wake up. I lived each day with the idea that if I'd stopped at the studio when I'd first noticed Phillip's truck, I might have saved Serenity before it was too late. Salinger actually tried to comfort me by stating that if I hadn't come along when I did, Phillip might very well have finished the job, giving Serenity no chance at all.

After he'd knocked me out, Phillip had set fire to the studio. If Zak hadn't seen my truck and come looking for me, we'd most likely both be dead.

As tough as my month had been, I'm afraid the people I love had endured even more difficult circumstances. Not only had Scooter been taken away and sent to live with his grandparents in Kansas, causing Zak a significant amount of angst as he worried about the future of the boy he'd come to care so much about, but we'd buried Lambda today after a long battle to save his life. Zak had tried so hard, but in the end the injuries he'd been fighting most of his life had taken over and weakened him to the point where his poor body could no longer fight the infection he'd suffered as the result of the fall he'd taken from Zak's back deck only days after my own brush with death.

As we drove home from the pet cemetery, Ellie had received a phone call from Rob, letting her know that he'd reunited with Hannah's mother, who was living once again in their old hometown, and wouldn't be returning to marry her as planned. I suspected Ellie was mourning the loss of Hannah more than she was the loss of Rob, but grief was grief, and my heart hurt for her.

And then there was Levi, who had never really recovered from Barbie's death. Sure, they'd broken up months before she was murdered, but Levi lived every day with the thought that if he'd agreed to meet with her as she'd requested, he might in some way have prevented what happened to her. Phillip was in jail after a long manhunt by the state police, as was the man we all thought of as lifeguard guy, but punishing the guilty didn't alleviate the pain of losing the innocent.

"We could all go on Ellie's honeymoon," I suggested. "Two weeks in Hawaii to relax and let our wounds heal."

"The house on the ocean is reserved from June 29th until July 15th," Zak agreed. "I'm sure Keoke wouldn't mind if we all stayed there."

"And there's plenty of room for all of us." Levi's eyes lit up for the first time in a month. "I'd love to do some diving, and it's been years since I've had the opportunity to surf."

"I did arrange for Kelly to cover the Beach Hut." Ellie dried her eyes and sat down on the edge of the sofa. "And I really could use some time away. It'd be nice to have a complete change of scenery."

"And school won't start for another six weeks," Levi added. "I don't have any plans for the summer."

"I've been itching to do some diving as well." Zak smiled weakly. "There's a wreck not far off the coast of Molokai that I've been wanting to check out."

"Two weeks in an oceanfront estate will give everyone time to gain some perspective," I offered.

"I'm in." Ellie smiled through her tears.

"Me too," Levi said.

Zak looked down at Charlie, who was still snuggled into his lap. He hugged Charlie and looked at me. "I can arrange for Charlie to come with us; do you have someone to watch the cats?"

It looked like we were all going on Ellie's Hawaiian honeymoon.

RECIPES FOR *BEACH BLANKET BARBIE*

Pulled Pork BBQ Cheese Fries

Salmon Wheels

Crab and Artichoke Dip

Potato Salad

Fudge Sundae Pie

White Chocolate Trifle

Pulled Pork Barbecue Cheese Fries

3 lbs. Boston butt pork roast, trimmed of fat
Sea salt
Black pepper
1 can beer or other liquid
1 to 1½ cups barbecue sauce
1 lb. seasoned frozen French fries
1 cup shredded sharp cheddar cheese
Additional barbecue sauce
Green onions, chopped

Season pork roast with salt and pepper. Place in slow cooker and pour can of beer (or other liquid) over top. Cook on low for at least 8 hours.

Once the pork is done, carefully remove from the slow cooker and remove all the visible fat.
Use two forks to shred the meat by inserting the forks into the meat and pulling in opposite directions.

Toss with barbecue sauce, adding enough to reach desired wetness.

Bake or fry the French fries as directed on the package and top with shredded cheese.

Broil until the cheese is melted and top with two cups of the pulled pork.

Drizzle with additional barbecue sauce and top with chopped green onions.

Salmon Wheels

1 can (14 oz. approx.) salmon, drained, bones and skin removed
1 package (8 oz.) cream cheese, softened
4 tbs. salsa
2 tbs. parsley
8 flour tortillas

In small bowl, combine salmon, cream cheese, salsa, and parsley. Spread about 2 tbs. onto each tortilla. Roll each tortilla tightly. Wrap in plastic wrap. Refrigerate 2–3 hours. Slice each tortilla into bite-sized pieces.

Crab and Artichoke Dip

8 oz. cream cheese, softened
8 oz. Havarti cheese, grated
2 cans (approx. 14 oz. each) artichoke hearts, diced
8 oz. crab meat, fresh or canned
2 cups Parmesan cheese, grated
1 cup sour cream
2 tsp. horseradish (add more if you like it hot)

Mix and bake at 450 degrees for 30–45 min.; stir after 20 minutes.

Serve with baguette slices, tortilla chips, or crackers.

Potato Salad

6 medium potatoes, boiled and skinned (boil in skin until very done. When skin begins to crack, rinse with cool water and then peel skin away; it should peel very easily.)
8 hardboiled eggs (I sometimes use up to 12)
2 cups mayonnaise
1 cup hot dog relish (yellow)

Combine in large bowl. Season to taste. I use Lawry's salt, pepper, and paprika.

Fudge Sundae Pie

Crust:
¼ cup light corn syrup
2 tbs. brown sugar
3 tbs. butter
2½ cup Rice Krispies cereal

Combine corn syrup, brown sugar, and butter in saucepan. Cook over medium heat until it boils. Pour over Rice Krispies. Stir together and then press into buttered pie plate.

Topping:
½ cup peanut butter
½ cup chocolate fudge sauce
3 tbs. corn syrup
(Note: I often make extra topping and pile it on thick. It's up to you.)

Mix together and spread ½ on piecrust. Layer in softened ice cream. I use vanilla, but coffee or chocolate works as well. Spread other half of topping over top.

Freeze for 2–3 hours.

White Chocolate Trifle

3 cups raspberries
1 prepared angel food cake

Filling:
1 cup whipping cream
3 tbs. sugar
4 oz. cream cheese
3 squares (1 oz. each) white baking chocolate, melted

1 carton (8 oz.) frozen whipped topping (such as Cool Whip)

Bake cake according to directions. Cut cake into cubes. Set aside.

Wash and sort raspberries. Set aside.

In a mixing bowl, beat cream until peaks form. Gradually add sugar. Beat until stiff peaks form. Set aside.

In another mixing bowl, beat cream cheese until fluffy. Add chocolate and beat until smooth.
Combine the cream and cream cheese mixture.

In a deep glass bowl, layer cake cubes and raspberries on bottom. Add filling layer. Add second layer of cake, raspberries, and filling. Top with frozen whipped topping. Garnish with raspberries.

Books by Kathi Daley

Buy them on Amazon today.

Paradise Lake Series:
Pumpkins in Paradise
Snowmen in Paradise
Bikinis in Paradise
Christmas in Paradise
Puppies in Paradise – *February 2015*

Zoe Donovan Mysteries:
Halloween Hijinks
The Trouble With Turkeys
Christmas Crazy
Cupid's Curse
Big Bunny Bump-off
Beach Blanket Barbie
Maui Madness
Derby Divas
Haunted Hamlet
Turkeys, Tuxes, and Tabbies
Christmas Cozy – *November 2014*
Alaskan Alliance – *December 2014*

Road to Christmas Romance:
Road to Christmas Past

Kathi Daley lives with her husband, kids, grandkids, and Bernese mountain dogs in beautiful Lake Tahoe. When she isn't writing, she likes to read (preferably at the beach or by the fire), cook (preferably something with chocolate or cheese), and garden (planting and planning, not weeding). She also enjoys spending time on the water when she's not hiking, biking, or snowshoeing the miles of desolate trails surrounding her home.

Kathi uses the mountain setting in which she lives, along with the animals (wild and domestic) that share her home, as inspiration for her cozy mysteries.

Stay up to date with her newsletter, *The Daley Weekly*. There's a link to sign up on both her Facebook page and her website, or you can access the sign-in sheet at: http://eepurl.com/NRPDf

Visit Kathi:
Facebook at Kathi Daley Books, www.facebook.com/kathidaleybooks
Twitter at Kathi Daley@kathidaley
Webpage www.kathidaley.com
E-mail kathidaley@kathidaley.com